THE BILLIONAIRE'S VIRGIN

PENNY WYLDER

Copyright © 2017 by Penny Wylder

All rights reserved.

No part of this book may be reproduced in any form or by any electronic or mechanical means, including information storage and retrieval systems, without written permission from the author, except for the use of brief quotations in a book review.

Sign up HERE!

1

———

I'm losing my mind. That's the only thought that sears through my brain as I crouch on the ratty, threadbare couch, staring at the website open on my ancient laptop. The screen is cracked in one corner, but unfortunately the distorted pixelation hasn't gotten bad enough to hide the hideous pink-and-gold banner at the top of the page.

Sugar Babies. The internet's notorious one-stop-shop for rich guys looking for hot young things, and vice versa. Now known for something else, too. A little side business that started trending among the profiles on this site.

This is what I have sunk to. Listening to Erin's utterly insane suggestions.

Hell, she hadn't even meant this one seriously—and Erin once in all seriousness suggested that I try selling my kidney, because she'd heard you only really need one, and the black market value was through the roof.

Her voice from the night before still echoes in my head. "You know there's a website where you can sell your virginity? I read this HuffPo article—one girl made *two million dollars.* Can you believe that? For one night." She'd laughed, and paused to toss back another healthy gulp from the water bottle-turned-wine flask she'd taken to carrying on nights out (because San Fran isn't like living in the backwaters of NoCal, and the bartenders always card). "I always learn about this shit like, four years too late, y'know?" She'd smirked around the lip of the bottle. "Hell, I bet even the kind of creep who'd buy me would've been better than fucking Jason McSwindle."

I'd raised an eyebrow, grinning back at her. "Don't you mean Jason McThimble?"

"Sure as hell felt like it!" she'd crowed, and then we toasted to bad first times and terrible dates and shitty kissers, and the whole conversation derailed. I'm sure by now, as she sleeps off her post-party hangover in the closet she rents (it literally used to be a walk-in closet, until our landlord Pano punched a hole in the wall, stuck a window pane into it, and called this a two-bedroom instead), she's already forgotten all about virgins-for-sale.

But why would she remember? Why would she even think it was relevant to tell me? As far as Erin, my best friend since sophomore year of high school, knows, I lost my V-card to Aaron Zimmerman behind the bleachers after senior prom.

I never had the heart to tell her the truth. That we got as far as his hand up my shirt and his somehow thicker-than-usual tongue down my throat and the hardwood gym floor absolutely killing my ass, not to mention a horrible cramp in my side from dancing my heart out with the girls earlier, when I asked him to stop. He was a total gentleman about it, which made me feel bad about being completely disinterested in banging him. I wasn't *that* naïve—I knew my first time would probably suck. I just wanted it to be a little less . . . Well. High school.

But Erin was so damn excited that I'd "finally joined the deflowered club," I didn't have the heart to admit nothing actually went down.

And now it's too late. Now I'm a nineteen-year-old virgin, living in Sin City as my grandmother calls it, and I'm too shy to even flirt back when a cute guy chats me up at work because I feel like it's written all over my forehead.

Never been fucked.

Virgin for life.

I first clicked open this website because, frankly, while Erin was exaggerating about some girl making 2 million dollars on here, she wasn't exaggerating by much. And God knows I need the money.

But the longer I stare at this homepage, the crazier I feel, because I'm starting to think it might be a good idea for more than just the cold hard cash.

I mean, yes, 99% of me wants the money. But that little 1% in the back of my mind is thinking, *I could rid myself of this brand for good.* I could be a normal 19-year-old again.

Not to mention I could finally satisfy my raging hormones. It's not for lack of desire that I've never gone to fourth base. I've got a hardcore imagination and a serious relationship with my vibrator, that's for sure. Finally stripping down with a real guy and letting him take control, touch me wherever he wants, position me any way he likes, and then thrusting his hot, thick dick inside me . . .

Shit. Am I actually getting turned on by the idea of selling myself?

Shy and paranoid as always, I shoot another quick glance at Erin's door. But it's still closed, and through the thin wood, I can hear the vague rhythm of her snoring.

"You're just looking, Bonnie," I murmur under my breath. "You aren't committing to anything."

I click through a couple of sample profiles to reassure myself. There are some hot guys on here—unless the samples are totally imaginary people. Which I guess is possible. But damn, if the real guys look anything like the blond hunk of half-naked on the first page, I could totally be down with letting him fuck me senseless.

Still, hotties or not, it feels like taking a running leap into an ice-cold pool when I click the little button next to the header that says Create Account. *Pretend it's a regular dating profile,* I command myself. After all, I've written one of those before. Erin practically forced me at gunpoint to make a Tindr account when we first moved here together.

"Just you and me conquering the world, girl," she'd declared. "And taking advantage of all the boys in it while we're at it."

Erin was a lot closer to world-domination than me—she was in her sophomore year at Fashion Institute of Design now, one of the top colleges for design and merchandising in the country, and well on her way toward a design degree that would make her bucketloads of money as soon as she graduated (albeit with a crazy amount of loan debt).

Me? I was just struggling to make ends meet, waiting tables in every spare minute I could find between studying my ass off for my nursing degree. A degree that was looking farther away by the minute, now that I had to delay a semester in the face of everything with Gram . . .

Anyway, at Erin's behest I'd created the damn Tindr profile, and then I just solved my embarrassment about it by deleting the app as soon as Erin looked the other way.

But this site's questionnaire is a lot harder to complete.

For one thing, it's *so long.* And for another, there are the questions themselves.

What's your deepest, darkest fantasy?

I pause, my fingers hovering over the keyboard. I think about my go-to daydream. A handsome stranger shooting me come-hither eyes at the bar. We barely know each other, but he crosses the room anyway, grabs me by the hand and pulls me into the restroom. Before I can blink, we're making out, hot and heavy. His hands are all over me, under my shirt, down my jeans. Circling my nipples, then pinching just hard enough to make me gasp, and slipping a thick finger into my soaking pussy at the same time. He shoves me against the wall, pins me there and pushes my skirt above my hips. I can't even see him, but I can feel his thick, fat cock rubbing all over my ass, teasing between my cheeks, before he finally thrusts deep inside me and starts to fuck me, hard and fast.

I swallow hard. My hand strays toward the hem of my jeans. My panties feel damp already and I'm only on the first damn question. Shit.

I take a deep breath. Somewhere out there, a guy is going to read this answer. A few guys, probably. But the thought of my future V-card owner reading this fantasy is what spurs me to be honest. Because the bathroom fantasy is only one of my usual imaginary pit-stops when I whip out the vibrator. I've got others, like that same mysterious guy bending me over a desk, or throwing me across a bed and repositioning my body however he wants. So I summarize.

I fantasize about a man taking control and training me in the bedroom. Or other rooms, I add before I hit enter.

Describe your sex life in one sentence.

Well, if I'm going for the virginity thing, I guess honesty

is the best policy. *Nonexistent,* I type. Okay, it said sentence, but brevity is the soul of wit, right? *Unless my vibrator counts,* I add.

If you could have one wish granted, what would it be?

That one, at least, is easy. *I wish Gram were healthy.*

But you can't exactly talk about real things on a website designed for selling yourself to the highest bidder. I purse my lips and stare at the page header again.

Sugar Babies: All that you desire, ripe for the taking.

I crack my knuckles. Right. I'm a smart woman. I aced my first two semesters of nursing school while holding down a full-time job. I'm surrounded by my bestie's whip-smart feminist badass friends on a daily basis. I can churn out academic essays almost as quickly as I can calculate a patient's BP. I can handle one silly website questionnaire.

I wish I understood my desires.

Hmm. Probably not the sexiest thing I could put, admittedly. But it seems like the right combination of honesty, insecurity, and maybe a hint at hidden depths. Plus, it's true. I don't always know why things turn me on. Why the idea of a guy fucking me doggy style with my face buried in a pillow, or shoving his cock down my throat until I gasp for air makes me wet. I want to try those things, but I'm a little afraid to admit it.

I take another long breath. Okay, maybe a few breaths. And a cold shower.

Finally, I reach the free remarks section, where you can write a couple of sentences about yourself. By now, the pitch is already lined up in my brain, half stolen from the articles I read about other girls doing this themselves, and half dredged up from those aforementioned depths.

I am nineteen years old, I write, *and I'm a virgin. I'm looking for the right man to claim my virginity, but only if the price is right ... After all, this cherry is a one-time only deal.*

I cringe at the last sentence, not least because it's something my grandmother once said to me (she's always been a little more-frank-than-feels-comfortable when it comes to discussing the birds and the bees). But hey, honesty and all that.

Besides, I tell myself as I click through the last steps of setting up my profile, adding a few of the cute selfies I have saved from my social media pages, along with a couple of full body pics of me dancing at a ballroom swing event and playing pool in Erin's dorm rec hall. *It's not like this is going to actually lead anywhere.* This is ridiculous. Those stories about other girls doing this *have* to be exaggerated. And even if a couple people did manage to get bidders on a site like this, nobody on here is going to notice *me*. There's got to be about a zillion hot ladies on here, all ripe for the picking.

I take a second to swap out the pool hall pic for a better angle—one where my ass sticks out at just the right angle as I bend over to take a shot. Hey, I might be a virgin, but I know my assets. Then I hit post, and wait for the load screen to pop up.

Your profile has been created.

"Bonnie?"

I practically jump out of my skin, snapping my laptop shut. But it's only Erin, yawning and tugging her closet-turned-bedroom door open. She's still wearing her miniskirt from last night, and a top that looks like it should be consigned to the trash by now, seeing as how it's more holes than fabric.

She blinks at me through raccoon-y eyes, and I hop off the holey couch. "Coffee?" I offer before she can ask what I was doing, because I can already see her eyes darting from my guilty, nervous expression to the closed laptop case and back.

That does the trick, luckily. "Oh hell yes," she manages before another yawn overtakes her.

I set the water on to boil and pull out the teapot we've been using as a makeshift French press. "Rough night?"

"You don't know the half of it." But she's grinning, even as she winces and eases herself onto the barstool in front of our kitchen counter, the only thing close to a table or eating space in our little 400-square-foot pad. "Remember Chaz?"

"The Art Institute's only football jock?" I snort. "How could I forget. I'm pretty sure he singlehandedly hit on every single girl at the Halloween party last weekend."

"Yeah, well . . ." Erin bites her lower lip, but fails to hide the sly grin that's started to emerge.

"Oh my god," I groan as I fish through the knee-high fridge for cream. "Tell me you didn't hook up with him."

She bats her eyelashes. "Okay. I didn't hook up with him," she says, laying hard on the didn't part of the sentence.

"Erin!"

"What? You've got to admit, player or not, he's a hottie."

"Sure, he's ripped and he has that whole . . ." I gesture at my face. "Easter Island thing going for him, but—"

"That whole *what*?" Erin bursts out laughing.

"You know, like his face is chiseled. And probably everything else, too." I smirk. "But his head is probably also made of stone."

"He goes to the Art Institute, it's not like he's a complete meathead—"

"You heard him at the party arguing with MaryAnn that having 5% alcohol by volume meant beer was stronger than vodka because the latter is 'only 40 proof,' right?" I raise an eyebrow.

"He was joking," Erin replies, albeit in an uncertain tone. "Besides, who cares if he's a math whiz? He knows his calculus, if you know what I mean." She wiggles her butt in the chair, and I groan audibly as I pour the now-boiling water into our not-really-a-coffee-press.

"If you stop punning, I'll stop making fun of you for banging the class musclebrain."

"Brains *are* muscles, Ms. I'm A Nurse," Erin grumbles. But she accepts the mug I pass her and bows her head. "But fine, no more puns. It's too early for braining anyway."

I glance at the clock over our two-burner stovetop. "It's almost 3pm."

"Exactly. Early." She yawns again, and pours herself a sip of coffee, even though it hasn't finished brewing completely. "Hey, isn't it Tuesday?" she adds a moment later, and my insides turn to ice.

"Oh, shit." *How could I forget?* I leap into action, racing across our living room to my own closet-slash-bedroom. It barely fits my little twin bed, and there's not so much a closet as there is an open hole in the wall where I stuck a clothes rack I stole from a Macy's dumpster. I yank my work uniform down—black skirt and black top, low-cut as per the manager's request, of freaking course.

"Relax," Erin calls, "The Bart is running fine."

Knowing her, she's got the schedule up on her phone right now, double-checking for me. But that's not the problem. I completely forgot that I promised Raul I'd cover his early shift today. Which means that instead of arriving at 5pm as per usual, I'm due at Big Daddy's in less than 45 minutes.

Luckily, I have more than a little practice getting ready

on the fly. I throw on my 'Got Milk?' shirt and skirt, grab my apron from the door and stuff it into my purse at the same time that I balance on one leg to tug on my sleek black flats.

"Fill me in on the meathead later?" I yell as I sail toward the front door.

"Oh trust me, you're gonna love the rest of the story," Erin calls back, just before I slam the apartment door between us.

It takes me ten minutes to jog to the subway, because we have to live way off the main drag to afford our place. Lucky for me, though, Erin is right—the Bart isn't delayed today, so I manage to sail into the restaurant with a minute to spare.

Pete, our slightly-less-creepy-than-the-owner-but-still-creepy-enough manager lurks in the window, scanning passersby like he's waiting for someone. When I jog past, his eyes light on me, and I realize he's watching for me.

"I'm on time," I say as I breeze past him toward the stockroom, where I can log into our time system. "Don't even try to convince me I'm not."

"Cutting it a little fine, huh Scrabble?"

I grimace at the nickname. Pete decided on my first day that my last name, Taylor, was too hard to pronounce. He took it on himself to nickname me after "a bad hand of Scrabble."

"What does it matter? I'm here; that's what counts."

"Being early shows determination," he counters. "It shows your dedication to this job; it tells me that you care."

Frankly, there's not another person in this diner who cares more than me, if that's our definition. Raul is pretty reliable, but most everyone else breezes in and out when they please. Aside from Raul, Pete, our owner and me, nobody else has lasted more than six months straight in this place.

But me, I'm going on two years now. "Gimme a break, Pete," I groan as I punch in my employee code and verify the timestamp.

"I will not." He crosses his arms, and I fight an inward grimace. I've touched another of his sore spots. Dammit. Me and my carelessness today. Why am I so distracted?

Unbidden, my mind drifts back to that website. To the profile I created, and the wish I let loose into the world. I can't stop thinking about the guys reading it right now. I imagine one of them getting hard, looking at my photos, thinking about doing all the dirty things I dream about to me . . .

But is this really how I want to lose my V-card, much overdue though it is? To some random stranger? Some stranger who *pays me for it*?

There is something strangely hot about that. It's so anonymous, so . . . businesslike. Wham, bam, thank you ma'am style. And a guy who will buy a girl's virginity from a site like Sugar Babies won't hesitate to be as rough with me as I want him to.

Is that even legal? I also wonder, a little too late now. And if so, does it make me any better than, well, a common . . .

Pete is still talking. I zone back in.

"—body is going to cut you slack. If you don't discipline yourself, you open yourself up to let other people do it for you. That's what I'm trying to teach you here. All of you," he clarifies, though from the way he glares down his nose at me, you'd think he meant only me, specifically.

I lift my chin a little, defiant. "I'm here on time, Pete. That's all you need to know about my personal life, thanks."

His mouth drops a little—that might be the first time in almost two years of working here that I've ever dared to speak back after one of his holier-than-thou sermons. It'll only make the rest of the night worse, I know—he'll be doubly determined to make me "respect" him now. But for the moment, I revel in my one small victory, and brush past him out of the stockroom to take my place on the floor.

It's going to be a long night.

2

———

Everything aches. From the balls of my feet all the way up to the crown of my head. I've pulled double shifts before, but last night we had one of those tables from hell—15 people who rolled in just before closing, and of course Pete made us seat them. We didn't get out of the restaurant, after doing all of our post-shift cleaning and restocking, until almost 4 in the morning.

Now, bright and early at the crack of noon, I needed to haul my ass out of bed and get onto a train north, if I didn't want to miss my chance at visiting hours today, my only day off.

I tug on my jeans as I flip open my laptop to check the train schedule, and suddenly there it is again. Staring me in the face.

Your profile has been created.

I highly doubt it's attracted any notice since I made it less than 24 hours ago—*if it ever attracts any attention at all,* a cynical part of my brain notes—but morbid curiosity makes me hit refresh.

Then I slowly sink into the couch, because my knees stop working.

372 notifications.

"Don't jump to conclusions, Bonnie," I mutter under my breath. That could mean anything, really. 372 guys might have made new profiles since I joined. They could be automated messages to let me know. Or just little notes like on social media profiles, nudging me to talk to someone or like someone else's photo to get started.

Really, could be anything.

But a little part of me knows, even before the notification page finishes loading, that it's not nothing. It's far from it.

Sure enough, the majority of the notifications are for messages sitting in my on-site inbox. Just a glance at the subject lines of those makes my stomach clench in a combination of fear and excitement, disbelief and a heady rush of relief. Because the subject lines all contain, for lack of a better term, bids.

"$15,000 for a taste of that sweet pussy," reads the first email, and they only get crazier from there. I scroll up slowly, not opening the emails themselves, not yet, because I'm not willing to even entertain that all of these are serious. They have to be pranks, right? Or if the guys are serious, they're probably serial killers or something secretly.

Shit, what the hell am I getting myself into?

But then one message in particular jumps out at me.

The numbers all around it have gotten seriously high, like, *I would actually consider that* high. Offers for $45-50k, just for one night with me, just for the opportunity to forever be labeled the first guy who got to deflower me. I can't decide if I'm flattered or nervous or turned on or freaked out or some combination of all four.

Part of my brain is already doing the mental math.

$50,000 would pay for one of the three months Gram would need at the good nursing home. The really nice facility I toured with my cousin Cam, the only other one Gram still talks to, as she and I debated options. The one that has personalized one-on-one nurses and on-site rehab, the one where they looked at her charts and didn't sigh in despair, but patted my shoulder and told me she's a strong woman, they could make her better. Give her another ten to fifteen years, depending how hard she was willing to work in rehab. And knowing Gram, she'd work her ass off if it meant getting her independence back.

$50,000 could change our lives. Give her a fighting chance. Maybe even *save* her life.

But then my eyes skim past that offer, because I've noticed another one. One that couldn't possibly be real. One with one extra zero, I figure a typo, surely. There's no other words in the subject line, no comment about my hot ass or my tight bod, or the way he wants to ruin me. But this sender didn't need any other words. He gets his message across in numbers alone.

$500,000.

My brain doesn't even bother trying to daydream about that one. *No freaking way.*

Still, my fingers seem to be functioning independently from my cerebrum. They're already clicking open that message, and my eyes scan the first line.

Bonnie.

Shit, I think immediately. Why did I use my real name? I probably should not have put that kind of detail up on a website like this. Scratch that, definitely should not have. Oh god, I am going to wind up with so many stalkers.

But something makes me keep reading anyway.

Your offer piqued my interest. I'm sure you have heard from a lot of other men already, given what you have to offer, but trust me when I tell you: I know what I want when I see her. And I do not make offers like this lightly.

If you are serious about this, you can find me on Skype at the below address. By the way, I would advise creating a more convincing pseudonym for that site, Bonnie.

I'm torn between blushing bright red and glaring at the screen. What an asshole.

I mean, he's right. But seriously, can he get any more condescending?

Don't keep me waiting, he has the nerve to add at the bottom of the email, right above his signature line. P, is all it says. "Or is that even your real name, Mr. Get a Pseudonym?" I mutter. His Skype username is PiercingPine32, so maybe it's a play on that? Who knows.

My finger hovers over the delete button. Surely some of these $40-50k offers will be from less irritating know-it-alls.

But $500,000. That could pay for as much time in the top-of-the-line facility as Gram needs. Not to mention the year and a half of nursing school I've already been through and the remaining two to boot. I could study full-time, maybe even finish in three years and start working earlier than I'd planned. Without juggling shifts at the diner, I could easily manage that.

I chew on my lower lip. I *am* on here to sell myself to the highest bidder, after all. And Mr. PiercingPine certainly is that. Who cares if he's the biggest asshole on the planet, if he'll pay me that kind of money for one simple night?

The least I could do is see if he's serious. Try to scope him out, see if he's a nutjob. He's probably just some broke kid from the Midwest fucking around on this site anyway, trying to see if he can get some girl to give him her bank information if he promises to send her money. Well. I might be a virgin, but I'm not exactly some naive little schoolgirl.

"Fine, P," I murmur as I pull up Skype and set up a new username: BonnieSeeksClyde. "Let's see what you've got."

The account created, I add PiercingPine32 to my contact list. I'm about to close the laptop again and head off to the train when my computer pings.

He added me back.

Was he just sitting around waiting for me? I raise an eyebrow. The broke kid in the Midwest theory is looking more and more believable.

My fingers hover over my keyboard, frozen as I try to think of an opening line, when his chat window pops up.

Took you long enough, my dear.

Long enough? I snort, then check the Sugar Babies site again. He only put in that bid an hour ago. He's lucky I checked it before I jetted off to Gram's, or he would have been waiting even longer.

Then again, maybe he would have just bid on some other hot virgin by then. If it's as big a trend as Erin seemed to think, there must be a ton of girls cashing in on this right now.

So I swallow my pride and my instinctively irritated response. Right. Sugar Baby. Virgin. Sweet, innocent young thing looking for a man to corrupt me. Get into character, Bonnie.

It's embarrassingly easy. After all, I kind of *am* looking to be corrupted right now. At least, if you call losing your V-card corruption. Which seems like a very Catholic school-girl thing of me to think.

"Progressive feminism, Bon," I mumble. Nothing wrong with wanting to get my pussy wrecked by a hot guy with a huge dick.

Sorry to keep you waiting, Mr. P. Or do you have a name? Mr. Pine?

My name is Pierce, Bonnie. I should return the favor, after all, one real name for another.

"Oh, like Piercing instead of Pierce is such a great disguise," I mutter under my breath. In the chat, I type, *How do you know that's my real name?*

Am I wrong? he counters.

I purse my lips. *No. I'm just curious why it was so obvious.*

Let's just say, your name wasn't a type of animal, flower, or fruit. It stood out.

Oh. I frown at my screen. *Sorry, I haven't done this before.*

Don't be sorry. I like that about you.

What, the things I haven't done?

I expect him to tease me, but all I get back is a one-word answer.

Yes.

Well then. Guess we know what his fetish is. Then again, that probably should've been obvious when he offered me half a million freaking dollars. I rub my temple with one finger. Okay. Time to figure out if this guy is for real.

So how does this work, exactly? I'm in the middle of typing, but another message from him interrupts me.

Enough small talk, Bonnie. I need to see you.

"Whoa, kidnapper much?" I raise an eyebrow. But, almost as though he's reading my mind, he qualifies that statement immediately.

Virtually speaking, of course.

Without another word, my screen lights up. I jump so hard the laptop nearly flies off my thighs.

He's calling me. Video chat. Not just audio.

My eyes dart around the living room. No way. Erin could come home at any time—I haven't got her schedule memorized, since it's pretty random during the week. I grab my laptop and bolt into my bedroom, shutting the door behind me.

But, of course, it looks like a time bomb went off in here. Between my late shifts at the diner, my classes, and being up in NoCal so often, I don't have much time to take care of the place. My bed is heaped with semi-dirty laundry, jeans and sweaters I can totally get away with wearing one or five more times before I need to haul them to the laundromat. My desk is piled with notebooks and print-outs and high-lighters scatter the floor.

I shove everything on the bed off of it and position myself in front of my least embarrassing poster, a simple reprint of Audrey Hepburn in *Breakfast at Tiffany's*, gazing soulfully out a window as a cig dangles from her gloved fingertips.

I suck in another deep breath and answer the call. For a second, my own camera feed floods the screen, and I bite the inside of my cheek to keep from grimacing. Shit. It's not just my room that looks a mess right now. I've got my blonde curls in a messy bun on top of my head, there's still smudged mascara from last night clumped around the rims of my green eyes, and I'm wearing Erin's freaking Fashion Institute of Design & Management sweatshirt, the old one she cut the shoulders out of and then got bored with.

Crap. Dead giveaway where I am, if this guy is a stalker. Not that I go there, but I live close enough for the shirt to be incriminating.

I'm in the middle of tearing it off when the call connects. Thanks to that, the first thing I hear from him is a low, throaty laugh.

I tear the sweatshirt the rest of the way off my head and

my eyes land on the computer screen. I freeze in place like a deer in headlights.

Definitely a scam, screams the only functioning part of my brain that remains. Because holy fucking shit.

He. Is. Smoking. Hot.

Icy blue eyes study me in high-definition. He's got the kind of cheekbones you could cut a steak with, and a strong jawline to match, complete with careless, dark two-day stubble that he clearly doesn't even notice is there. It only serves to highlight his perfection, like shading on an art drawing. I imagine running my hands through that scratchy stubble, feeling it rough against my fingertips, my palms, my own cheek . . . Or between my thighs.

"Tell me, Bonnie," he says, and fuck, this is unfair. His voice is deep, full of charcoal, with some kind of New England accent that I can't quite place. Maine? Boston? No, fancier than that. Connecticut, maybe, or Vermont? "Do you always begin your video calls with strangers by stripping?"

I swear, my cheeks could start a small forest fire.

"Uh . . ." I clear my throat, hard. Ugh, it's not fair. He's got a full head of dark hair. The razored edge in front flips over his forehead, just low enough to skim his equally perfect black eyebrows, which are currently arched in amusement. "I forgot I was wearing . . ."

Then I glance at myself on cam. Great. Underneath the FIDM hoodie, I had the wonderful fashion sense to don a bright red T-shirt with the Trix rabbit on it. Super sexy, Bonnie. Meet the hot rich man with a cereal shirt on.

"I'll be right back," I say. "I'm just going to change really—"

"Sit down," he says, because I had started to rise. I freeze halfway to my feet, laptop in my hands. His ice-blue eyes lock on mine, and I remember the hint of command in his messages earlier. Part of me prickles at him trying to order me around.

Another part of me, a much larger part than I want to admit, is turned on as hell by the calm control in his voice. This is the kind of man who tells people what to do. This is a man accustomed to being obeyed. One who won't be afraid to take control, to dominate me.

This is not the kind of guy you ignore.

I sink back onto my bed, laptop balanced on my crossed legs. "Whatever you say, Pierce." I lock eyes with the camera, and I swear I can *feel* him looking at me through it, a palpable sensation.

His smile turns predatory. I don't know how to explain it —it's the same look he wore a moment ago, only now the edges of his mouth seem sharp, his blindingly white teeth flashing, his eyes hungry. "I apologize, Bonnie. I seem to have given you the wrong impression."

I blink at the screen. "What do you mean?"

"You asked me my name. It is Pierce. But that is not how you will address me. You will address me as 'sir.' Is that clear?"

Again, I'm torn. Half of me wants to rebel, to tell this asshole to shove it. The other half, my lower half, tingles in anticipation. Fuck. I can already feel my panties starting to grow damp. "Yes, sir," I whisper, and it makes me feel even hotter to hear those words come out of my mouth.

"Good girl. Now, Bonnie. I'm not one for beating around the bush. Are you interested in my offer?"

"Very," I blurt. Shit. Do I sound too eager?

He raises an eyebrow, and sits in silence. It takes me a moment to realize what I've forgotten.

"Sir," I add belatedly.

He nods. "Better. And I'm glad to hear my offer caught

your attention. I hoped it would. As I said, you piqued my interest. And I have rather, shall we say, exacting taste." His gaze slides down my body, and my face burns again as I glimpse the stupid bunny on my shirt.

Dammit, Bonnie. I can't even sell myself properly.

But he's not frowning. He's still got that hungry smile on when his eyes snap back to mine. Or at least, to the camera, which makes it feel like he's staring straight into my soul. Those eyes of his are mesmerizing. So pale they're almost gray, except for the bursts of bright blue around the center.

"I hope this arrangement will work for both of us. But I understand, of course, that there will need to be certain parameters set. And certain proofs given."

"Proofs?" I repeat like an idiot. Then I shake myself. Of course. "I mean, yeah, I . . . No offense, but I don't really know if you're who you say you are, so—"

He raises a single eyebrow. "Who did I say I was, Bonnie?"

I blink. "Er. No one, I guess. What I meant was, I've never met anyone from the internet before, and, uh, well, you hear stories about . . ."

His smile deepens. "I understand completely. Naturally, I will provide you with whatever proof of trustworthiness you require, along with a small token of my means upfront, to assure you of my honest intentions. You will, I trust, be willing to provide the same type of proof to me."

"I . . ." This was not at all how I pictured this would go. Then again, I hadn't expected it to actually *go* anywhere. "Yeah, of course," I stammer.

"Bonnie," he says, and there's a warning in his voice that I don't quite understand.

"Yes, Pierce?" Shit. Only then do I realize. "I mean, sir. Sorry, sir.

"That's the second time you've forgotten." His eyes flash. "Don't do it again."

Fucking hell. Why is it so damn hot when he does that? And why do I want to simultaneously slap him and press my lips to that perfectly sharp, curved mouth of his? "I won't, sir."

"Now. If at any time you begin to feel uncomfortable with this arrangement, or pressured in any way, you are free to walk away. I want you to remember that, Bonnie. None of this is necessary. It must be something you want to do."

"I do, sir," I reply, my voice strong and clear. Because I really do, I realize. For the money, but also to lose my virginity once and for all. And, additionally, because Pierce P here is literally the hottest man I've ever spoken to for more than 10 seconds. And the way he's devouring me with his eyes right now, like I'm a piece of meat he's hungry to bite into . . . Fuck. I want him to do whatever the hell he wants with me. Money or no money.

Focus, Bonnie. Eyes on the prize.

"Same goes for you," I tell him, suddenly. "If you don't want to do this or anything, or change your mind before we . . . Um, before we do that. I understand, sir."

He laughs, and that sound, low and almost dangerous, does funny things to my stomach. I feel like I just swallowed a jar full of butterflies.

"May I ask what's funny, sir?" I venture, my cheeks still red hot. They've been burning this whole time, an involuntary reaction to him. Just another reason to be embarrassed. Between that and my hideous shirt and my complete awkwardness, it's a wonder he hasn't ended this call yet.

But his eyes rake over me again, still every inch as appreciative. "Oh, my dear. I thought my desire was quite clear." He's doing that thing again, staring straight at me, and the computer seems to melt away, so it feels like we're in the same room, face-to-face. "I want you," he says, and I swear to god I can feel my leg muscles start to give out. Thank god I'm sitting.

Once again with the mind-reading, however, he tilts his head to the side. "Now, Bonnie. Please stand. I'd like to see all of you."

I rise on trembling legs, and the laptop is at an angle on the bed where it just points straight at the crotch of my jeans.

"Move the laptop. Do you have a desk?"

Why am I letting him order me around? I wonder, even as I obey and set the computer on my desk. Much better angle, though it shows off my messy room behind me, and the fraying window curtain and tape-marked walls behind that. Oh well. He wants to know what he's getting.

"Take off your shirt."

I feel my nipples harden beneath it, and a throb of desire pulses straight to my crotch. But I hesitate, one hand on the hem. "Look, no offense, but I still don't really know who you—"

"What is your email, Bonnie? Preferably one without a last name in it; you can't be too careful online."

I tell him my secondary email, the one I mostly just use to sign up for spam newsletter lists and sales announcements from my favorite stores, since it's not like I can afford to shop in any of them anyway. I watch him click on his screen a couple times.

"Check your inbox."

Blinking, I turn away to shuffle through my belongings for my phone, which wound up under the pile of laundry in my haste to clear the bed. I stand and refresh that inbox, then stand there like a dumbass in the middle of the room, gaping.

There's a $300 Visa gift card in my inbox.

"As I said. A small token." He raises that damn eyebrow again. "Now. The shirt?"

I should feel dirty. I should feel cheap. I should not feel this fucking hot while stripping for a guy who just threw cash at me. But fucking hell, I feel like a sex goddess as I peel that Trix shirt off of my body and let it drop beside me. At least I wore a decent bra today, leopard print with black straps. Push-up, too, so the girls are on full display. I don't have much of a chest, but what I do have fills out an A-cup to almost overflowing, and gives me a nice curve of cleavage.

Pierce seems to agree, from the way his eyes graze my skin. I feel hot everywhere he looks, set aflame. I've never had a guy look at me like this before. It's more than simple desire, more than *I want to tap that*. He wants to take me, possess me. Use me in ways I probably haven't even imagined.

I want to learn exactly what he has planned for me. Already I can feel myself getting wet between the thighs.

"How's this, sir?" I lean toward the camera, smiling right at the lens. "Do you like what you see, sir?"

"Speak only when I ask you to," is his only reply. "And take off your jeans, too."

I unbutton those, and shimmy out of them. The underwear doesn't match the bra, but it's cute too, a narrow little red cheeky number. Thank god you can't tell from the camera's point-of-view that said panties are already getting damp. I wouldn't want him to think I'm too easy.

Or would I?

"Turn around," he says, and I immediately spin so my back faces the camera. "Slower," he barks.

I rotate slowly, swaying my hips as I do, peeking over my shoulder to study his reaction. Unless I'm mistaken, he's breathing a little faster now, leaning closer to his screen. His pupils have dilated too, and he can't seem to tear them from my ass.

That is, after all, my best feature. I've got a narrow waist, and fairly small chest, but I more than make up for it with my hips and ass. Especially in these cheeky panties. My butt is muscled and pert and I can already imagine his hands on it, squeezing my ass as he pulls my body against his hard chest. Thinking about it, I can't help running my hands over my hips, letting my fingers trail over my tight ass, pretending it's him.

He exhales sharply. "Turn back around."

I obey.

"Have you ever had sex with a man, Bonnie?"

I shake my head. "No, sir."

"Why not?"

It takes me a second to recover from that blunt question. "Uh. I guess . . . I never found the right guy. And then it was too late."

"What do you mean too late?"

I grimace. I didn't mean to say that. "I mean, too late to lose it casually, you know? It became a big deal that I hadn't, and then it seemed weird—"

"Stop that."

I freeze, unsure what I've done. "Stop what, sir?"

He points. "Crossing your arms."

I didn't even notice I had. But sure enough, I'd crossed my arms over my chest, and started to hunch in on myself, self-conscious about being semi-naked in front of this guy. I force myself to unfold them, slowly, and press my palms against my thighs to keep them there.

"What about women?" he asks.

I blush. "No, sir. I don't swing that way, sir."

He smiles sideways. "You never know." He winks, and for the first time since we started talking, I glimpse a real person there, behind this confident, sexy conversationalist. Then he's moving on, swiftly, to the next order of business. "What about fingering. Has a man ever finger-fucked you?"

I flush. "No, sir."

"Have you kissed a man?"

"Of course. I mean, yes, sir. A couple."

"Did they get under your shirt?"

"One, sir."

"And did he fuck those pert little tits of yours?"

If I thought I was red before, it's got nothing on me now. "I . . . How do you even—no, sir."

He's chuckling softly, eyes crinkled at the edges in genuine amusement. Well, at least someone is enjoying making me uncomfortable.

To be honest, though, now that I'm in my underwear, I can feel the faint breeze in my room against the fabric of my panties, and I am acutely aware that he's not the only one enjoying this. I'm even starting to relax a little, adjusting to being mostly naked on camera. I look fucking hot, judging by the little corner of the screen that shows me his view.

I wonder vaguely if I should be nervous about baring it on cam. But it's not like guys haven't seen me in bikinis before. That's as much fabric as I'm wearing right now. If he asks me to go any farther, I think I'll hesitate. Videos like this get leaked of girls all the time, circulated to their friends, their teachers . . . *Their grandmothers,* I think, and it takes every ounce of effort I have not to flinch.

Gram would literally die if she could see me right now. So, no complete nudity on cam.

Thankfully, without me needing to say so, Pierce seems to sense that's a line I won't cross. Unfortunately, he seems much more interested in baring me verbally before him. "What about your ass? Has anyone fucked that gorgeous ass of yours, Bonnie?"

"N-no, sir." Fuck I am so wet right now. The idea of anal terrifies me, but hearing him talk about fucking me so straightforwardly . . .

"Good. Have you had a man's cock in your mouth? Have you ever licked a man's balls, or wrapped those perfect, sexy lips of yours around his dick?"

"No, sir," I breathe. Suddenly I'm finding it hard to keep my voice even. My heart is beating rabbit-fast, and the tingles have spread from my stomach all the way down to my toes.

"I'm glad to hear it, Bonnie. Do you know why?"

Thud. Thud. Thud. My heart beats so loud it's a wonder he can't hear it through his speakers. "Why, sir?"

"Because I am purchasing your virginity, Bonnie. If you agree to this contract, that means I get to take every single virginity you have. You will be mine, until I have taken what I want. Do you understand?"

"Yes, sir." My nipples actually ache, they're pressing into my bra so hard. My knees are trembling, and not from fear anymore.

I have never been this turned-on in my life.

Still, my mind keeps darting back to the questions he asked. About anal. About oral.

"But . . ."

"Are you still interested in pursuing this contract with me, Bonnie?" He cuts me off. "Be very sure of your answer. I want you to want this as much as I do." His eyes bore into mine. I couldn't look away if I wanted to, and oh, I do not want to. "When I fuck you, Bonnie, I intend to make you come so hard you forget your name. You will enjoy yourself. You will fucking love it. And when I am finished fucking your mouth and your ass and your pussy, and when I've made you cum enough to please me, you will be paid in full. But I am doing this for my pleasure. Your number one priority will be pleasing me, for the duration of our contract."

"I understand, sir," I reply through trembling lips. What am I saying? Have I really thought this through? And what does he mean, *all my virginity*? "I just have some concerns . . ."

"Naturally," he says. "But you must understand. This is a one-time offer. All or nothing. That's what I'm paying for."

Don't do this, screams the sensible half of my brain. But the blood has all flooded from my brain to my pussy now, and it's not really my sensible half calling the shots anymore.

Besides, even my sensible half is desperately, painfully aware of how much I need this money. Not just for me. For Gram. For my future, for school. Hell, with that kind of dough, I could swing for an apartment for Erin and I next year where we don't have to fend off roaches on a regular basis.

I swallow hard, trying to wet my suddenly dry tongue. "I want to do this, sir. I want you to . . ." I trail off, hot in the face.

"Say it. Tell me what you want me to do to you, Bonnie."

I swallow hard and lean in close to the laptop. "I want you to fuck me," I whisper.

Bang bang bang.

I leap back from the computer like I've been scalded,

yelping. But it's only Erin outside, pounding on my bedroom door.

"I come bearing Starbucks," she yells. "Get it while it's hot, Sleeping Beauty!" She starts to turn the knob, because we have a pretty casual "come in unless there's a scrunchie hanging on my doorknob" policy (and of course, the only scrunchies around here have been on her door, not mine).

I leap across the room to catch it and hold the door shut. "Be out in a second!" I shout, my voice strangled and tense. "Just changing real quick."

"My bad. Be in the kitchen," she calls back, and her footsteps creak off across the living room. I sag against the door with a gasp of relief.

That's when I hear Pierce's laughter again, and I realize the speakers are far too loud now that Erin is home. I dart back to the laptop to quiet him, and find him smirking at me. He's enjoying this way too much, the bastard.

"I am based in San Francisco. You are in Oakland, I understand?" he adds nonchalantly, getting right back to business, and I gape at him again.

"How did you . . . ?"

"The FIDM sweatshirt." He grins. "I love a girl who prioritizes education."

I narrow my eyes. "Yeah, well. Don't judge a book by its cover. I don't go to FIDM."

"Doesn't mean you don't prioritize your education, does it?"

I roll said narrowed eyes. But I shake my head, sighing. "Fair point, I guess. Sir," I add, slightly sarcastically.

His smile widens. "In the future, when you sass me, it will cost you."

Feeling emboldened by his desire, and by standing in my lingerie in front of a webcam for the last ten minutes, I lean in toward the screen. "Oh really?" I grin. "Is that a threat or a promise, sir?"

His eyes widen, and so does that sharp smile of his. "I have a feeling I'm going to enjoy my time with you, Bonnie. Very, very much."

The pulse of desire radiates throughout my body, until I feel it from the top of my head all the way to my fingertips. I want him. Oh, fuck, I want him bad. My heart slams against my ribcage, nervous and excited and panicking all at once.

"One more thing. Before we meet, I would like you to have your pussy waxed. Full Brazilian."

My mouth drops open. That was not part of the bargain.

But he talks right through my shock. "Go to the Luxe Gold Salon in downtown San Francisco. Tomorrow at noon. They'll be expecting you." He smirks again, and that smile has probably caused whole legions of women to fall to their knees before him. "The salon manager will have your instructions following that. And don't worry about your . . . wardrobe." His gaze darts to the corner of my screen, clearly eying the pile of clothes I've got stacked there. "I'll send something over for you to wear."

Before I can protest, because there's oh so much to protest—how does he know I'm free tomorrow at noon? What does he mean I need to get a *full Brazilian* just so he can fuck away my V-card? And what the hell does sending something for me to wear mean? —he's ended the call. I'm left staring at a black, empty screen, with a thundering pulse, and an absolute puddle between my legs.

He might be hot—okay, ridiculously so, which is definitely a bonus when it comes to agreeing to fuck him—but he's a cocky asshole, too. Adding on all these caveats last minute—I have to get waxed, I have to wear some suitable outfit he chooses, because nothing I own could be good enough for him, clearly. Two can play at that game.

He wants to pay for my virginity, and he'll get it. My regular virginity. Normal sex, nothing else. Nothing kinky or crazy. If he's making me rip out all my pubic hair just to fuck him, it's the least I can stipulate.

I stand in the middle of my room, formulating this plan, staring at my blank computer screen, for at least a few minutes. Until I hear Erin shouting from the kitchen, something muffled about coffee break. Then I snap back to attention and pull my jeans back on, nabbing my discarded shirt.

What have I gotten myself into?

3

———

"How are you feeling, Gram?" I hold her arm as she makes her third circuit of the gardens outside the temporary home where she's staying, which is already costing me an arm and a leg every night. At least that price comes with certain privileges, like how I bullied my way in to visit even though technically I missed visiting hours (thanks a lot Pierce with the spontaneous and distracting webcam call).

I don't even want to think about the loan bills racking up with every day that she remains in here. Not to mention the credit card I had to charge my rent to last month.

"I told you, Bonnie, I'm feeling fine," she grumps, because it is the third time I've asked her, to be fair. But according to the nurses, she was anything but fine today. Her PT session was a disaster, and there was a particularly scary moment where she forgot her general practitioner's name, a man she's known for at least five years.

I can't even begin to think about losing her. I know she's getting older—it's inevitable. And I know that one day, I'll need to face a world without her in it. But I can't bear the idea. She's my only family left, since Mom passed, and my father was never in the picture. She raised me from the time I was eight years old. She's the only real parent I've ever known.

I can't lose her. Not yet.

But she's also never been one for talking about being sick. Or admitting she's human. Even when she had pneumonia once, when I was fifteen, she ignored the symptoms and kept working. Right up until she collapsed in the middle of a shift at the hospital. Her supervisor forced her to take 3 days off, but after that she was right back up and at 'em, saving lives and helping people.

She's the reason I decided to become a nurse. Trailing around after her at the hospital was where I first fell in love with the idea of helping to care for the sick.

Carers don't like to let people take care of them, I guess. Against their nature. I squeeze Gram's arm tighter. "Just listen to the doctors, okay? And take it easy when they tell you to. They told me about you wandering around after curfew, you know."

She huffs. "Well it's ridiculous. I'm not a child. I'm a grown-ass woman who can take care of myself."

I stare at her pointedly. "And *why* did you leave the ward at three in the morning, Gram?"

That huff turns into a sigh. "I was craving gummy bears from the visitors vending machine."

"Right. Sounds very grown-up," I tease with a smirk.

"When did you become such a smart aleck?" she grumbles. But she's smiling, so I know she doesn't really mind. "Anyway, enough about me and my old bones. Tell me about yourself. Your stories keep me young at heart." Her eyes twinkle as she smiles up at me.

Up. Because she's shrunk in the last few years, not because I've grown. We used to be exactly the same height,

5'4", and I loved that. Now I feel abandoned here, as she's shrinking away.

I shake myself to attention. "Oh, not much. Work is as miserable as ever. Paul's still a jerkwad."

"And school?"

"Going okay." I shrug, feeling a pang of guilt. I haven't worked on prepping for my next exam, and it's in just a week and a half. I really need to get on that. "I guess a little hectic. But nothing new."

"This is not keeping me very young." Gram clucks her tongue. "No exciting adventures or wild nights out with Erin? No suspicious young men I should be interrogating or threatening, hmm?" She grins, and I groan and turn my head away.

Mostly to hide the flush across my cheeks. *Oh yeah, Gram. This hot new guy, total asshole, who I'm about to sleep with for a bucketload of money.*

That would go over great.

"I shall take that as a negative." Gram shakes her head. "Well, all's the better I suppose. You can't go getting distracted from your studies, not now. The right man will come along when you least expect him. Until then, you're smart." She pats my arm with a smile. "Keep your eye on the prize, and everything else will work itself out."

Oh, Gram. I am keeping my eye on the prize, trust me. But the prize, for me, would be keeping her whole and healthy as long as I can.

I'm not ready to navigate this crazy world on my own yet.

* * *

"Right, what's going on?"

I freeze in the middle of the living room, as the kettle

whistles from the stove. It's been twenty-four hours since I first met Pierce. Well, "met" via the computer, I guess. And already I'm about to head off to let some strange woman get all up in my business, seeing parts of my body no one else has, just to please him. I wonder if he convinces every woman he fucks to jump through this many hoops?

Thinking about those wolfish eyes of his, and that predatory grin, it's not hard to imagine. I'm pretty sure every woman on the planet would say "how high?" if he told them to jump.

But, I haven't exactly mentioned any of this to my room-mate. I force a huge smile and face Erin. "What do you mean?"

She smirks. "Well, I wasn't sure. Until you put your guilty face on just now." She takes a running leap onto the couch, sending my laptop bouncing through the air. "Tell me, Bonnie! Are you quitting your job? Starting a secret business empire?" Her smile turns sly and knowing. "Is it a boyyyyy?"

"It's nothing!" I protest, snatching the kettle from the stove as it continues to whistle at a deafening pitch.

"Bullshit. You were closed in your room talking to someone yesterday, now you're up way before noon, when I know for a fact you don't have classes today and you don't start your diner shift until 7 tonight."

"Do you memorize my schedule, you creeper?" I laugh, back still turned to her. I wonder how much more noise she'd be making just now if she found out I called out of my shift tonight, asked Raul to cover. It's the first time I've called off of work in the entire time I've worked there. Normally I work right through sick days. But I faked vomiting sounds on the phone, and I guess Paul was afraid enough about the potential for cross-infection with the food that he let me switch. Projectile vomit and waiters do not make for a healthy combo.

"You've only had the same one for a year." Erin splays across the couch. "Not my fault I'm observant."

"Well, observe your own business," I call over my shoulder. But by the time I've poured the tea, I turn around to find her full-on pouting at me. Puppy dog eyes and all. Shit. I can never resist those.

"Come on, I share all my good stories with you. Even the embarrassing ones! I told you about hooking up with *Chaz*, for chrissake."

"Okay, okay." I huff. "You don't have to guilt-trip me." I hold up my steaming mug of tea and another bare palm in the universal sign of surrender.

"So it *is* a guy!" Erin squeals and sits up on the couch, clapping her hands. "Who is he? Where'd you meet? What's he like?"

"We haven't met yet!" I protest. "It's probably nothing. I don't know."

"Oooh, a hookup? Has our sweet little Bonnie finally decided to slut it up?" Erin leaps off the couch to catch my shoulders and size me up. I'm in my usual jeans and a tighter T-shirt than usual, but nothing special. After all, Pierce is dressing me up like his personal doll anyway, so why bother?

Erin tsks, though. "If this is a first date, you can't go looking like that. It screams *desperate dork*."

"Gee, thanks. I wonder why I didn't tell you anything." I snort and swat at her hands.

"At least let me do your makeup," she protests. There's that pout again.

I sigh and roll my eyes, though secretly I love when she fusses like this. "Fine, but nothing too weird."

"Just some blush and subtle lips, I promise!" She bounds toward her bedroom. "Maybe some mascara," she calls over her shoulder. "Hmm, or eyeliner too . . ."

I sigh again and check the clock. "Fine, but I only have twenty minutes. Then I need to run."

"Wow." Erin returns with a scarily large makeup bag in tow. "Early for a date. This gonna be an all day thing, or does he work nights?"

I shrug again. This earns me another sigh.

"There's nothing to be ashamed of, you know," she tells me as she paints a pale pink gloss over my lips. "Everybody needs to get laid now and again. We're not Puritans. Hookups are perfectly normal. There, how's that?"

But as I check myself over in her hand mirror, admiring the subtle way she brought out the green in my eyes and made my skin look smoother, more uniform and less prone to blotchy red blushes, I wonder how normal she'd think this situation was. Being a virgin at 19 is weird enough. Agreeing to lose it to some guy from the internet might be a little more usual nowadays, I guess.

But getting paid for it? Oh hell no.

So I just smile, close-lipped, and thank my best friend for her help.

"Well if you won't give me his name, at least let me know where you're going," she demands as I'm throwing on my coat to leave. "If he's from online, he could be anyone, y'know."

I pause at the doorway, relenting. She's right. "I don't exactly know yet . . ." I admit, wincing when her eyes widen and her mouth drops open with a million more questions. I raise a hand to stem the tide. "It's a surprise. But I'll text you as soon as I find out, I swear. If I don't message you by two, feel free to send out the search parties."

She salutes. "Aye, aye, captain." Then she melts into a wink. "And hey, Bonnie? Do me a favor. Have some fucking fun, will you?"

* * *

So far, I am failing in my promise to Erin to have fun. There's nothing enjoyable about lying spread-legged on a sterile white table in a colorless room while a strange woman sticks her head between my legs. And that's before the hot wax.

I flinch as a huge glob of the searing hot stuff lands on my nethers. I've got my fists clenched at my side and my teeth gritted in preparation, but honestly, that wasn't so bad. I crack an eyelid to peer up at the woman, an Amazon of a redhead who looks like she could twist my leg off as easily as de-hair it.

"Was that it?" I ask, starting to breathe again. That wasn't *so* bad. After all the horror stories I've heard about waxing, I was expecting way worse, to be honest.

"No," Red snaps.

The next thing I register is white-hot, searing pain. It's accompanied by a horrifying ripping sound—I mean, I get the whole process in theory, but I didn't expect it to sound like Velcro being torn open. Luckily, I'm so shocked by the stab of agony in my delicate flowery bits that I don't remember to scream in pain. Tears sting the corners of my eyes, though, and my palms have four crescent moons dug into each one in red, where my nails cut my skin.

"That was," Red says.

"Jesus," I gasp, starting to sit up.

She shoves me back down onto the bench. "I did not finish. That was the first strip," she clarifies.

Fuck my life.

Four more agonizing bouts of that, to clear all the hairs between my ass cheeks, down my thighs and across my faint happy trail. By the fourth one, I'm not as shocked anymore, so I remember to yell.

"Sorry," I mumble, after shouting at what felt like the top of my lungs. Definitely loud enough to hurt my throat.

"Don't be," Red replies gruffly. "It's better to let it out." She slaps my tender pussy with a huge glob of liquid heaven. I flinch from the slap, but relax at the cooling sensation of whatever magical moisturizer she's applying. "Healthier to scream, I always say."

"None of this seems particularly necessary for health," I groan between clenched teeth, though the cream is starting to cool the burning sensation at last.

I'm starting to wonder if $500k is going to be worth all this after all. I mean, what's next? A full-body scrub with sandpaper? Carving off any moles or blemishes? Boob implants? Who the hell knows where this all ends.

Though, I have to admit, when the Amazon leaves the room, indicating I can get dressed again, and I slide off the table to check myself out in the mirror, it does look very neat and tidy. I run a hand between my legs and marvel at the baby-smooth skin. It's still bright red, angry from the wax, but the red is fading already thanks to the miracle lotion.

Without thinking about it, my fingers drift to my clit, massaging it gently. As they do, as I watch myself in the changing room of this fancy as hell salon, after being molested by a burly Irish woman, all I can think about is the way Pierce looked at me on camera yesterday. Those ice-blue eyes devouring every inch of me. His parted lips and the steel in his voice when he ordered me to stand up. To strip.

I remember him telling me what he wants to do to me. *When I fuck you, I will make you come so hard you forget your name.* I can hear his voice now, the surety in his gaze. That man gets what he wants. Always.

And what he wants right now is me . . .

My fingers stroke across my clit in a slow, circular rhythm. My lips part, and I gaze at myself, naked in the changing room mirror, trying to picture what Pierce sees. My pert breasts and my tight waist. I run my free hand over my hips, up my stomach to circle my nipples. With my other hand, I trace the lips of my pussy, feeling a drop of moisture there as I start to breathe faster.

I imagine him standing behind me, watching me touch myself. His hard eyes on my bare pussy. I picture him wrapping his arms around me from behind and stroking me, teasing me with his fingers. I close my eyes and my hand becomes his, toying with my clit, so close to touching the hard little sensitive spot at the tip, but never quite getting there. Dragging this out as long as he wants.

Pretty soon I'm sagging against the mirror, heart pounding as I finger myself harder, faster. My clit feels so sensitive, my pussy tight and wet with desire, every muscle in my body tensed in anticipation as I race toward a climax . . .

Clatter clatter.

The doorknob of the dressing room starts to turn and I gasp and leap away from the mirror to grab my clothes. I'm holding my jeans and shirt defensively in front of my body when the Irish Amazon re-enters, her small eyes squinting over at me.

"Sorry. Thought you'd be dressed by now." She steps inside the room anyway, and I guess it doesn't matter since she's already seen my formerly hairy vagina. She sets two fat store boxes down on the bed, each one wrapped in gold ribbon and tied in a bow that Gram would've killed to be able to imitate for Christmas presents. "Forgot to pass these on earlier—these are for you. Also, there's a car waiting out front when you're ready."

I nod a reply. Something about the mute confusion on my face must strike a nerve with her, though, because Red pauses before leaving again, her eyes on mine.

"Be careful with his type," she says, her gaze all too knowingly sharp. "They'll eat you alive if you let 'em."

Before I can ask what she means, she's gone, the door to the room slamming shut behind her.

Has Pierce sent girls here before? Has he had other virgin sacrifices prepped this same way, before he had his way with them?

I shake my head. Of course he has, Bonnie. Don't be crazy. There's a reason this mad rich man is willing to pay an insane amount of money to sleep with you. It's because this is what he gets off on doing.

I try not to worry too much about what that means, what it makes me to accept his money, as I turn back to the bed and undo the ribbon on the first box.

My jaw drops.

Okay. Not what I was expecting. I figured he'd want me in a slutty schoolgirl getup, or maybe some kind of frilly, doll-like dress. Instead, I unfold a gorgeous black silk gown from within a fluff of gold tissue paper. It's floor-length, with a slit up one side, tasteful yet just revealing enough to tantalize. The neckline is similar, dipping low enough that it would show only a hint of cleavage, if I had much to display. It's a sleek, modern style, the kind of gown you see on red carpets or in the Who Wore It Better sections of celebrity gossip rags.

Not the kind of gown you wear to a paid hookup, I think. Then again, it's not like I know anything about hookups, paid or otherwise.

The second box catches my eye. When I lift it experimentally, it feels a lot heavier than the first one. Huh. I undo the second ribbon and open the lid to reveal two separately wrapped bundles. Within the first, heavier bundle, I discover a pair of black and gold heels. They're not sky-high, thank god, because I don't know if I'd even make it to the door of this changing room wearing a pair like that, let alone out the front door. But they are at least 3 inches tall, and narrow. Not quite stilettos, but real honest-to-goodness heels, nothing like the cork wedge sandals that are the closest thing I own to heels.

I bite my lip gently. No worries. I'll figure them out. They are gorgeous, too, and the soles don't look killer. When I stick a finger onto the pad, it feels soft and supportive, not like a lot of cute but deadly shoes.

Then I catch a glimpse of the brand and freeze in shock. Louboutin? I may not have known exactly how to spell that until this very second, but I can guarantee these babies aren't knock offs.

Shit.

I swallow hard as I untie the other tissue-wrapped package. Then I burst out in a grin. This is more what I was expecting.

A silk-smooth matching set of lingerie falls to the changing table. There's a thong, if you can even call it that, since it looks more like a string of dental floss mated with a patch of lace. And then there's the top, black just like the panties, lace as well as lace-up—it's a full bodice, complete with a bustier designed to give my girls a solid push. I check the size tag hesitantly, worried I might have given Pierce the wrong impression with the bra I wore on cam.

But no. It's exactly my size. 34A, a little big on the A-side, but not quite large enough to slip into B territory. When I shimmy into the bustier, it feels like putting on a hug. A really tight, slightly uncomfortable hug, but one that lifts my girls onto full display, cupping them just right, and hugging my curves the same way. The panties are a perfect fit too, and even though I shouldn't be surprised by this point, I do still lift my eyebrows when I slide the gown over top, because holy shit.

Not only does Pierce have flawless taste, but he's also got a dead eye for a lady's size. The thought of him memorizing every inch of me, figuring me out down to the centimeter, is sexy as fuck. The man pays attention to everything, every tiny detail.

The gown hugs my waist and flares out over my hips, giving me a gorgeous hourglass figure, emphasizing my chest without crossing the line into trashy territory, and dipping low in the back to show off the nape of my neck and the spot where my shoulder blades meet.

Even the fucking shoes fit. Jesus. *How did he figure out that one*? I wonder, until I remember that when I arrived at the salon this afternoon for my preparatory body massage and wax, they asked for my shoe size. I'd figured the masseuse needed it for some reason, but now I realize that Pierce must have asked them to relay that information and selected these shoes at the last minute.

However he managed it, I'm impressed. And the rest of the measurements, the salon didn't ask for those. He must have been able to size me up just from those few minutes we spent chatting on cam . . . Which tells me exactly how closely he was paying attention to every inch of my body.

In spite of myself (and my close call earlier), I can feel a faint pulse of desire in my pussy. Again. Damn. I'm going to get these nice, sexy new panties all wet before I even meet up with Pierce.

Oh well. I have a feeling he isn't going to complain. And whether it makes me crazy or not, I have to admit, a part of me is seriously enjoying this. I'm his doll, his plaything, and he's dressing me up however he wants. And apparently, he is in to some really fancy dolls.

I slide on the heels and they're actually pretty easy to walk in. Supportive but sexy all at once. I twirl in the mirror for a moment, admiring my new look before I stuff my old clothes, which in comparison to this outfit look like something out of a Goodwill donation box, into my oversized purse. Thank god for San Fran sized bags, which we need to pretty much live out of, since no one here can afford a car to throw their extra necessities into. My clothes fit easily, and the slouchy hobo style bag still looks fine, albeit a little bit out of sync with the rest of my outfit.

Then I stride out of the changing room, feeling like a million bucks.

Well, okay. Half a million bucks. Soon to be all mine, baby.

I flash Red a bright grin, and she shakes her head in despair, though I notice she can't help but crack a smile, too. "This sugar daddy of yours has taste, I'll grant him that," she tells me as she waves me on out, adding, "Don't worry honey, it's all pre-paid for. The car's out front."

But I linger by the counter anyway. "Did, um . . ." My cheeks flush. I don't really know the protocol for waxing, but I feel sure that if any beauticians deserve a tip, it's the ones who get all up in your private parts. "Can I leave a tip?"

Red laughs, loud. "Oh, sweetheart, you're adorable. He covered that too, but thank you for asking." She winks, and I guess that's that.

Time to face the music.

I take a deep breath and cast one more glance over my shoulder at my reflection in the salon mirrors.

"You look amazing," Red reassures me. "And if he don't appreciate that, well . . . You know where to tell him to stick it." She grins, but for all her compliments, it's clear she doesn't have a high opinion of my mystery man here.

What if she's right? What if this is all a huge mistake?

But I remind myself of Gram. Of school. Of the angry texts collecting on my phone from my manager because I missed *one* day of work after years of being the only reliable employee. Of all the reasons I'm really doing this.

Eyes on the prize, Bonnie, I remind myself, and then I square my shoulders, lift my head high, and march through the front doors of the salon.

4

———

I expect Pierce to be waiting for me outside, but instead I find a valet, full suit and everything, holding open the door to an idling limo. I mean full stretch limo, not just the shorter versions you normally see downtown because let's face it, who can fit a stretch limo on San Francisco streets?

Pierce can, apparently.

I smile awkwardly at the driver as I slide into the seat. It's leather, which normally isn't my bag (freezing cold in winter, hot and sticky in summer, who likes that?!). However, I can tell the moment my butt connects with this seat that it's better thought-out than your average car seat. It cups my body, and the leather is butter-smooth beneath my palms. It's only early fall, not even chilly enough for a jacket yet, though at least the summer heat has finally relinquished its grip. But there's a pleasant hum of warmth beneath me.

Mm. Heated seats.

I settle in and make myself comfortable as the valet shuts the door. I stretch my legs out in front of me and study the interior of the car for clues as to the man who hired it.

He's not here, so he must be meeting me wherever we're heading. I'm alone in the car except for a small sideboard bar, the booze stocking it all on display. I don't recognize any of the brand names, they're all unpronounceably foreign, but I can tell an expensive stash when I see one. Vodka from what is probably Russia to judge by the lettering, a bottle of champagne from France, a red wine from Italy, something called mezcal from Mexico I guess, since I can almost read the label for that one. Heck, even his whiskey is in a foreign language, Gaelic probably. And there's glasses beneath the bottles, cut to perfection, like little handheld diamonds that glitter in the limo's interior lighting.

So he likes his drink, but only the best of it. Got it.

My eyes sweep the rest of the interior, but aside from the smooth seats (and enough space that I start to wonder if this limo is larger than my bedroom at home), there's nothing else personal in here. My man of mystery remains mysterious.

Hmm. That or he rented this car just to show off. I lean my head back on the seat and study the ceiling. Did he choose this car for me specifically? Was it like the lingerie, carefully planned, or the dress, tailored exactly to fit me?

Maybe he plans to fuck me in here later, after wherever this car is taking me . . .

I trace my hands down my hips, loving the sensation of the smooth silk against my skin, brushing on my thighs and gliding beneath my palms.

Before I know it, my hands have drifted close to the outline of my panties. I tell myself I'm just checking the seams, to see if the thong is visible through the fabric of the dress. But soon I can't help pressing one finger flat along my mound, then another, inching toward my aching clit.

I can't stop thinking about him. About the way he reads

me so easily, terrifyingly fast. About the way he knows my body better than I do, able to judge my size and shape at a single hungry glance.

My fingers reach my pussy, and I press through the dress, rubbing gently, feeling myself grow wetter with each rotation of my hand. Fuck. Is this how he'll be touching me soon? Will he take the time to tease me, touch me, make me gasp for more, before he finally plunges his hard cock into me and strips away my virginity?

Or will he just grab me and have his way with me the second I walk through the door of . . . Wherever we're going?

I can't decide which fantasy I prefer more. Maybe the latter, because there's something desperate and visceral about it, imagining a guy like Pierce, a guy in control of everything around him, unable to control himself over me.

Somehow, though, I already know it won't be like that. He will be in complete control, that much I'm certain of.

He'll be in control of me, too.

All too quickly, the limo pulls to a stop. I haven't finished, and my clit throbs in protest, but I ignore it as the driver opens my door. It's probably better if I'm already a little horny going into this anyway. After all, what if I pull another prom night and freak out?

This isn't high school, I remind myself. And right now, I'm about as far from crouching under the bleachers with another inexperienced kid as I can possibly get.

I stand at the door to one of the nicest restaurants in the city. I know the name, of course, because anyone who's anyone in service, even down to the dishwashers, has heard of this place. The creme de la creme of elite society dine here every night, and although I heard a rumor that the French fries are actually just McDonald's fries shipped in at 3am every night under cover of darkness, everything else you could imagine ordering here is apparently to die for.

"He's inside?" I ask the valet as I step from the car.

The man smiles. "On the roof, miss."

I tilt my head back to spy the rooftop, a few dozen stories above my head. Before I can get too dizzy, a maitre'd from the restaurant opens the door, and next thing I know I'm being whisked inside, up an elevator. "Top floor," he says, needlessly, since he pushes the button for me. Then he steps out of the lift, and I'm alone with my thoughts.

Luckily, I don't have much time to start to panic. The elevator slows to a halt, the doors slide open, and . . .

I forget to keep breathing.

The elevator opens directly onto a rooftop, which is empty save for one sweetheart table, two chairs side-by-side, settled beneath a heat lamp against the faint chill in the night air. Beyond the rooftop, even just from this angle, I can see half of the San Francisco skyline glittering in the late afternoon sun.

Closer at hand, however, is what catches my attention.

Pierce stands beside the table in a jet-black three-piece suit—or maybe it's a tuxedo? I can never remember the difference, but he's wearing a bow tie and cummerbund beneath it, whatever it is. The sharp contrast of the white shirt and black suit make his ice-blue eyes pop even more starkly. He has just enough color in his cheeks to suggest he recently returned from somewhere much warmer than San Fran in the fall. And his hair, so dark on cam that I hardly saw it, is cut to fall just so over his right eyebrow, one of those *I just fell out of bed like this* looks that you know must be planned, and yet, it's so convincing that I really believe he didn't try too hard to style it that way. For a second he looks otherworldly, too attractive to be real, like a man who stepped out of a TV series into the real world.

Then my feet remember how to function, and I step out of the elevator, still staring mutely like an idiot.

"You must be Bonnie," he says, and holy hell, it's a good thing he didn't send me higher heels. It's hard enough to keep my balance at the sound of that deep, sexy voice of his, almost a growl in itself. "You look lovely, my dear."

"Sir," I reply, all I can think to say. Instantly, I hate the way I sound in comparison, so high-pitched and young. "Um. You look great too, sir," I manage. Ack. Why am I so awkward?

Oh, maybe because I've never had a billionaire rent out a private rooftop in preparation for defiling me before. I swallow, hard, past the nervous lump in my throat.

"I trust your morning went well." There's a faint smile on his lips, and a knowing tease in his voice.

"As well as possible, considering I was being tortured for half of it," I respond with a sarcastic smile of my own.

His grin only deepens. "Believe me, Bonnie, you don't know the meaning of torture."

A shiver races down my spine and settles deep in my body, centered somewhere around my already-damp panties. Damn him. "I trust you'll remedy that shortly, sir," I respond with a toss of my hair, stepping around him to slide into the seat he draws out for me.

"You seem quite comfortable," he remarks as he takes the seat beside me. We're close enough that I can feel the heat radiating from his skin, and his arm almost brushes mine, not quite, but close enough that the hairs standing on end on my forearm touch his coat sleeve. "Are you positive you haven't done this before?" His eyes catch mine, cock-sure and confident as hell.

Fuck, I wish it was easier to breathe around him. "I'm glad I fake it well." I arch one eyebrow, but there's a telltale quiver in my voice, and I curse myself for it. I didn't want to seem weak.

He seems to enjoy it, though. "There it is," he responds, his voice nearly a purr it's so soft. Then he snaps his fingers, and the sound is so startling on the quiet rooftop that I jump in my chair. "Champagne please," he says without taking his eyes off me, and for a second I think he means for me to serve him, until I notice movement out of the corner of my eye. A waiter appears, also in a suit, and carefully fills two flutes with champagne.

"Would you like to see the menu, sir?" the waiter asks, and Pierce shakes his head. He still won't take his eyes from mine.

Which means I still can't catch my breath.

"We'll have the chef's choice."

"What's the chef's choice?" I ask, as the waiter steps away from the table.

Pierce shrugs one shoulder. "No idea. That's part of the fun. Being surprised."

"Ah," I reply, not quite sure what else to say. I'm the kind of person who reads the whole menu three times over before I decide what I want, and even then I second-guess myself half the time.

"So." Those eyes scour my body again, pausing to linger on my chest before he catches my gaze again. "Tell me who you are, Bonnie."

"Er . . ." I procrastinate by taking a small sip of champagne, but it doesn't help. I shake my head a little to clear it. "I'm a student, studying to be a nurse in—"

"I didn't say tell me what you *do*," he interrupts. "I said tell me who you are."

"Well, I'm an Aquarius." I grin as he rolls his eyes. "And I also think zodiac signs are kind of bullshit, before you say anything else." He laughs at that. "Hmm, and . . ." Who am I? Why is this so hard to articulate? I force myself to look away from those piercing eyes of his, and study my empty plate instead. "I'm the kind of person who takes an eon to decide on my entree at restaurants, and then no matter what I choose, I have food regrets."

"Noted." He smirks.

"And, I . . . I'm kind of an introvert. But I like being around people too. Ambivert maybe? Like, I enjoy parties and meeting new people and making new friends, but I need recharge time in between to be alone and get my head on straight again."

"Sounds pretty normal to me."

I shrug.

"That's it?" he asks when I fall silent again.

"Well, it's a hard question," I protest.

"Those are the only kinds of questions worth asking, if you ask me."

I roll my eyes. "Okay, fine, Pierce, who are *you*, then?"

"An egotistical and eccentric man with a penchant for corrupting nice young ladies such as yourself, probably because I was corrupted at an early age myself and thoroughly enjoyed the experience. I'm an acquired taste, but I try to make up for that by ensuring that anyone who spends too much time with me is rewarded, shall we say . . ." His fingers brush my inner forearm, ever so lightly, the barest touch on my naked skin, but it makes my whole body stiffen. I almost gasp in shock at the rush of electricity that flows through my body. "Pleasurably."

My mouth has gone too dry to swallow. Probably because all the blood in my body is headed south right now.

Focus, Bonnie. I refuse to let him overwhelm me this easily. "So, what you're saying is you're kind of an asshole."

He laughs again, louder this time. I like his laugh, to my surprise. He seems to open up then, like the rest of this front he puts on is an act, but when he laughs, that's when I catch a glimpse of the real person underneath all the show . . .

"Precisely," he agrees when he's finished laughing. "What about you, my dear?"

"Am I an asshole?" I raise an eyebrow, torn between amusement and offense. "I really hope not. I'm sure my friends would have mentioned by now if I was, though."

"Do you have a lot of friends?" His hand is still on my arm, resting there now, and the pressure of his fingers is driving me wild.

I've never felt like this before. So electrified by a single touch. It makes me even more resolved—this is a man who's used to getting whatever he wants from everyone he knows. He may be buying my virginity, but he's not buying every inch of me. I steel myself against the desperate fluttering sensations in my stomach. "Only a few, but the ones I do have, I've had forever. I couldn't ask for a better crew."

"And your family?"

That helps shut down the butterflies. "It's just me and my gram."

"I see." There's something in his eyes that makes me think he might know a little something about that.

I shake my head, not wanting him to get the wrong idea or feel bad about me. "It's fine. Like I said, I have my friends. They're my family, really."

"So, you're a well-adjusted young woman, with good friends, and you're in school apparently . . ." That hand dances up my arm, touching the crease where my elbow bends, his fingers caressing the sensitive skin there. "What made you decide to sell yourself?"

I jerk my arm free, startled. "I'm not—" I start to protest, then cut myself off. Because, of course, I am. Technically. "I mean . . . It's not . . ."

"I'm not judging you, Bonnie." He stares at me, every inch sincere. "How could I possibly, if I'm willing to buy in? I'm merely curious what made you decide to take a step like this, especially if it will be your first time with a man."

"I've had boyfriends," I huff, still indignant, though his response helped a little. "I just . . . Didn't want to do anything beyond kissing with them."

"Why not?"

I shrug one shoulder, imitating him earlier. "I just . . . It never felt right. I've been imagining my first time for so long. I want it to be memorable. Not just some throwaway night, with someone who . . ." I pause before I finish. Because that was the real problem, wasn't it? *With someone who won't take charge.* My boyfriends were vanilla-baked, sweet and home-grown. They wouldn't take what they wanted from me. They wouldn't bend me over and mercilessly fuck me until it was hard to walk straight.

Pierce's eyes search mine for a moment. "I can promise you, Bonnie, you won't forget this." His hand rests on my arm again, light but somehow still possessive. "I will give you the night you want."

Oh, I am damn sure he will. And that thought is almost as terrifying as it is thrilling. I squirm in my seat. This is getting too deep and conversational. I came here to get rid of my V-card, not talk or make connections. Shit. I frown. "It's okay. I mean, I don't . . ." I huff out a sigh. "Can we change the subject?"

"Certainly." He laughs softly, and I can't help but resent

him. Even more so when his eyes dart down to my crotch. "How does your pussy feel, now that it's smooth as silk?"

As if in response, it clenches, a pulse of desire rocketing through me. I shift in my seat, uncomfortably aware that he turns me on way too fucking easily. "I was thinking of another subject." I press my palms flat to the table, hoping that will disguise the way they've started to shake a little. "When are you going to pay me?"

"Straight to business, hmm?" He smirks. "I like that in a woman. If you're so eager, we can get right down to it now."

My eyes dart around the empty rooftop. All I can think about is the waiter who was just here a moment ago, and the many buildings around us, with hundreds of windows facing our way. How many dozens of people would see if we went at it right here?

"But . . ." My gaze darts toward the door again, and he seems to read my mind.

"It will be fine."

"You can't know that," I say. "What if he comes back, or someone looks out their window? We could get caught."

His smile widens, sharklike, the way it did on camera yesterday. "That just makes it all the more exciting, no?"

"You don't worry about getting into trouble?" I raise an eyebrow.

"I think I could avoid any sort of real trouble, my dear," he responds pointedly.

"I . . ." Damn. He has me there. I'm sure he could buy his way out of any sort of fines for public indecency he might incur. But could I?

Then again, with the money he's offering me, yes . . .

But what if someone took photos or something? He's rich enough that someone might find it worth their while to sell photos of his hookups somewhere, maybe one of those gossip sites. I have a horrible flash of my grandmother stumbling across a picture of me in flagrante delicto in one of the gossip rags she devours, and my whole face heats up bright red.

"Not out in the open," I mumble.

"My mistake. I thought you wanted to get this over with." His eyes positively sparkle with mirth. He's enjoying himself, the bastard.

"Don't you?" I counter. "You've bought your goods. Don't you want to enjoy them as soon as possible? Get this over with and move on to the next conquest?"

His expression darkens, goes serious. "When I purchase an expensive meal, I do not inhale my food. I take it slowly. Savor every bite." His hand touches my shoulder now, and lightly pushes my sleeve off my shoulder, so the dress sags down my chest a few inches, revealing my collarbone. His fingers trace that, slowly as promised, like he's memorizing every inch. "I want you, Bonnie. But I want to enjoy owning you. I want to take you one piece at a time, and make you cry out in pleasure every step of the way."

My heart beats so fast I'm surprised he doesn't hear it, or at least feel it in his fingers, which now trail across my chest toward my exposed cleavage. It takes conscious effort to breathe, to keep myself from begging him to take me right now. I'm not even sure if it's because I want to get this over with, anymore, or if it's just because his touch, his voice, those self-assured words of his, are making me hot as hell.

He leans in closer, and my lips tremble, anticipating the feel of his rough mouth against mine, the scratch of his stubble on my soft cheek. But he tilts his head, brings his lips beside my ear instead, and whispers, his breath hot on my neck as he does. "If you really are so eager, though, I'll oblige. If you want to get this over with, I'll take you into the bathroom right now. Bend you over the sinks and fuck you, hard and fast. Someone might hear us, of course, especially as I intend to make you come on my cock at least, oh . . ." His hand reaches my cleavage, and he drops a finger beneath the neckline of my dress to trace circles around my nipple. "At least five or six times, before I'm finished with you. You'll be screaming by the time I'm finished."

I'm breathing hard now, not even bothering to hide it. I couldn't if I tried. My whole body arches forward, my chest pressing shamelessly up against his hand.

"But if you are set on moving forward now, then very well. I'll make you beg in the public restroom here, and if we're overheard, oh well . . . If you want my cock that badly, it simply can't be helped."

My face must be bright red by now. I turn to face him, reaching for him almost without thinking about what I'm doing. But he pulls away. Turns in his seat to face the rooftop, his pose as casual as if we'd just been chatting about the weather.

Only a glance at his crotch reveals that he's as affected as I am. He's hard as a rock, straining against the zipper of his pants.

"Maybe . . . Maybe not," I stammer, finally, now that I can think straight, without his hot breath in my ear. "Maybe we should wait until later." Then my stubborn side kicks in. I won't give him the pleasure of totally throwing me off guard. "Or not, I mean. Up to you." I lift my chin, calling his bluff. He said he wants to enjoy me. Savor me. He won't ask me to fuck him right here, or in some restaurant bathroom. No way.

But to my surprise, he tsks softly, still smiling. "Ah, Bonnie. Now you've gotten me all worked up." When his eyes flash back to mine, I see desire. They've gone darker, more dangerous. Hungry. "I told you, all of your firsts belong to me." He glances pointedly at the table.

Under it. "Let's start with the easy one."

Oh, hell. My cheeks might have been red hot before, but now it feels like my face could start a forest fire. "Are you . . ." He's laughing softly, enjoying every second of my shock and discomfort. Oh hell, *no*. Two can play this game. I lick my lips, slowly, and lock eyes with him. "What would you like me to do, sir?"

His hand slides down my arm to cup my fingers in his. He spreads my fingers with his own, and draws my hand over until I'm cupping his cock. I can feel the hard strain of him through the fabric of his dress pants, pulled taught now with his need. Fucking hell. My fingers stretch around him, and keep going, and going. His dick is long, yes, but also *thick*. I swallow a little nervously. Will that even fit in my mouth?

He doesn't give me more time to think about it. His other hand finds my shoulders, gently presses me down, off my chair, toward the floor. "I want you to put my cock in that pretty mouth of yours and suck. I want you to swallow every drop of my cum."

My pussy clenches again, reflexive. I'm getting wet just listening to him. Fuck.

Almost without thinking, I slide off my chair and drop to my knees. The rooftop floor is wooden, a little hard beneath me, but not unbearable. It's got some flex and give, and as I duck under the table, thanking god for the tablecloth that hangs almost to the ground beneath it, I find the position isn't as uncomfortable as I thought it would be. The fabric of my long dress bunches under my knees, provides a cushion as I kneel between Pierce's legs. He spreads them, and guides my hand to the zipper of his crotch, but he doesn't need to. My fingers are already working at his top button, undoing his fly. My mouth waters in anticipation. He wraps his other hand around the back of my head and digs his fingers into my hair, roughly, and I gasp, surprised by how much I enjoy it.

I draw his cock out of his fly, and take a second just to stare.

He's as thick as he felt, wide enough around that my fingers don't fit all the way around his girth. I run my hands up and down the velvety smooth skin that covers his steel-hard shaft, and smile to hear his faint, appreciative groan above the table. I lean in and lick him, slowly, starting at his base and trailing my tongue along his underside, all the way to the tip. A drop of precum hangs there already, and I lap at him, savoring the taste. He tastes exactly how he smells, masculine and heady and just a little salty. That surprises me, too. I like the way he tastes.

No, not like. I fucking love it.

I lick him again, let my tongue explore every inch of him, curling over his shaft, my hands sliding along his length at the same time. He lets me do that for a while, until his cock jumps in my hands, tensing with his desire. Then his fist tightens in my hair, and I know what he wants.

Closing my eyes, hoping I'm doing this right, I part my lips and let his cock glide into my mouth. I'm nervous, seeing how large he is, but he fits after all, and my lips close around his shaft as the tip of his cock inches farther into my mouth.

I lean forward, take as much of his dick as I can between my lips, my tongue pressed flat against the underside of his shaft, one hand wrapped around the base of his cock.

"Grab my balls," he murmurs above me, and I reach my other hand down to cup them. "Harder."

I squeeze gently, rolling them between my fingertips as I start to rock back and forth, pushing his cock out of and back into my mouth in a slow rhythm.

"Good," he says, and his voice is almost a sigh. "Now deeper."

I tense with nerves, but he doesn't give me time to worry. His fist clenches around my hair, pulls me farther onto his cock than I thought possible. I feel the head of him almost at the back of my throat, and for a second I almost panic, but I hear his voice again.

"Relax."

I let myself go. Let him take total and complete control of me. He pushes and pulls me, rocking his hips in tune with the motion, thrusting into my mouth.

"You like that?" he says, low enough that I can hardly hear him through the table. "You like having my dick in your tight little mouth?"

I groan around him, trying to agree, and he sucks in a sharp breath through his teeth. I moan again, slower and longer this time, so he can feel the vibration in my throat along his cock, and his hips buck against me with pleasure.

"You are a fast learner, aren't you?" he manages between gritted teeth, and in response I move quicker, wrapping my hands around him as I suck him harder. It's getting me so fucking wet to hear the suppressed quiver in his voice, to feel the way his cock bucks in my mouth and his body tenses beneath my fingertips. For this moment, I am in control of this cocksure, confident man, and I am fucking loving it.

"Sir, your first course."

We both freeze at the sound of the waiter's voice. I have my lips wrapped around the head of his dick, my hands in his pants, and I'm too freaked out to move an inch. I can't even breathe. To judge by the long pause from Pierce, he's having a similar problem.

Then, "Thank you," he replies, and somehow his voice sounds smooth as silk again.

That vengeful drive of mine kicks in. No way is he going to get away sounding all sweet and innocent when he's the one who talked me into this position. I flick my tongue along his shaft, twirling it around his head, and grin as his hips jolt slightly.

"Would you like me to wait until the lady returns? It is best served immediately."

"She shouldn't be . . . long," he finishes after a slight pause, one that probably only I noticed. But it's enough to make me go at him faster, rocking my head back and forth again, drawing his cock as deep into my mouth as I can stand and back out again, slow, my tongue teasing him all the while.

"Very well, sir. Would you like more champagne?"

"That would be lovely, thank you," he responds, to my horror. Shouldn't he be trying to get rid of this guy? Or does he *want* to get caught?

I dig my nails into his upper thighs a little, and feel his hand clench around my hair in response. I suck harder, move faster. His cock is a solid, trembling mass of tension now.

I listen to the waiter's footsteps—how did I miss them last time? —and the distant sound of him opening the champagne bottle, pouring Pierce a slow glass. All the while, Pierce keeps his fist in my hair, his hips arched, his cock rock hard.

"Anything else?"

"That will be all, thank you."

Footsteps cross the roof again, and I pump him harder,

forcefully. A door slams somewhere in the distance, and almost exactly at the same time, Pierce grips my head with both hands and thrusts all the way to the back of my throat, groaning as he comes.

I tense and start to gag at first, but he holds me in place. "Swallow it," he hisses, and his breath is tense with ecstasy. "Swallow my fucking cum."

So I swallow hard, and when he releases his grip on my hair, I keep going, sucking him in and out of my mouth, lapping up every drop of him, because fuck, he tastes good. I didn't expect that. I didn't expect any of this to feel so . . .

Hot.

When he finally sags in his chair, his hands still tangled in my hair, I slide out from under the table and retake my seat beside him, smoothing my hair, which I'm sure he's fucked into a tangled mess.

His eyes catch mine, bright with humor. "You have a little . . ." He touches his chin, and my face lights up red as a fire engine.

I grab my napkin to dab at the corner of my mouth, feeling the small trickle of his cum there. Oh my god. I'm still trying to wipe it clear when the door to the roof crashes open again and the waiter prances out with a jug of water.

I drop my napkin to my lap like he's just seen me clutching a murder weapon. My face still feels hot as hell, and I wonder if it's obvious from my disheveled hair and puckered lips what's been going on here.

The waiter refills our glasses, eyes on our untouched plates. Right. The appetizer. My eyes dart to it, widening. Pierce has already taken a few bites of his, though when he had time to, I don't even know.

"Is there anything wrong, miss?" the waiter asks, all innocent concern.

I duck my head so he won't notice my deepened blush.

"Yes, Bonnie, are you still hungry?" Pierce catches my eye, and it takes every ounce of self-control I possess not to kick him under the table.

"It's great, thank you," I murmur, not daring to breathe again until the waiter turns to leave us with our replenished water glasses. Only then do I snatch my fork and take a stab at the plate in an effort to distract myself.

Somehow, I need to survive the rest of this dinner . . .

5

———

"Thank you again for joining me," Pierce says as he shrugs on his overcoat. We're in the lobby downstairs, having finally finished the dessert course.

My stomach still feels half empty, probably because I had trouble eating anything with all the sideways comments and underhanded dirty jokes Pierce kept throwing my way. Anytime I finally started to relax and enjoy myself, he'd make sure to trail a finger up my inner thigh, or lean over and ask if the steak we were both having went well with my first course of cum. It's like he couldn't stand to sit at a table with a non-blushing girl for more than ten seconds at a time.

That, or he really enjoyed making me turn bright red in embarrassment. I'm leaning toward that latter theory.

But I notice him slip the coat check girl a fat wad of cash as she helps me into my coat, so maybe he's not an entirely horrible person after all? After my years working at the diner, I know by now that you can't judge a book by its cover —only by its willingness to tip the help.

The nicest looking people stiff me entirely on a bill,

leaving 10 cent tips on a $75 check. And then the grumpiest seeming assholes will leave me a 30% tip with a smiley face drawn in the margins. You never know.

So, against my better judgment, when Pierce rests his hand on my lower back and steers me outside, I follow him to his car. Sure, along the way I gulp a few deep lungfuls of fresh air, but that's only to gather my courage. Because this is it. This is the moment I've been waiting for.

It's time to lose my V-card, once and for all.

No limo this time. Just his personal car, a BMW, because of course it is. He holds the door for me, a true gentleman to the last. But service has taught me not to take that too seriously, either.

I slide into the front seat and perch on the edge of the leather seats like I'm about to drive a gauntlet. I do have to admit, though, his BMW is comfy as hell on the inside.

Pierce slides into the driver's seat, and I force myself to ease back in my seat and strap on my belt. No sense getting so worked up yet. We have to drive to his place first.

"So, did you enjoy sucking my cock, Bonnie?" he asks as he turns the key. Like he's asking about the weather.

I squirm in my seat. "Yes, sir."

He smiles. "Good."

Maybe he wants to fuck me in this car. The seats are roomy enough, and all the windows except the windshield are tinted. If we pulled into an alley, no one would notice.

Then again, that might go against his "I want to savor the fine meal" policy.

But to my shock, a moment later, he pulls onto the road, then glances at me. "Where do you live?"

Panic seizes me. All I can picture is Erin's face. Erin eyeballing me as I lead this handsome, way-too-well-dressed man into the closet I call my bedroom. Erin listening through our parchment-thin walls as we fuck, and he talks about taking my virginity . . .

I tell him the cross streets, then panic as he shifts the car into motion and starts to drive. Shit. "I can't do anything at my place though," I blurt, cheeks red all over again. "I . . . I have a roommate. Uh . . . She's very Catholic." Double shit. I'm babbling. But hey, technically she is Irish Catholic, even if she doesn't so much practice anymore . . .

And I can't exactly admit the real problem. Which is that I'd die if anyone found out I was doing this. Selling myself. Selling my *virginity,* which all of my friends think I've long since lost anyway.

But Pierce just laughs, loudly. "Relax, Bonnie. I only want to take you home." His pale blue eyes catch mine, twinkling with mirth as he shifts lanes. "Well, okay. I *want* to do more than that. But tonight I'm only dropping you off."

"Why?" I blurt. Then I realize with a mental kick how rude that sounds. I clear my throat. "I mean, why wait? Don't you want to, you know . . . I trail off, and he raises his eyebrows, waiting for me to finish. I clear my throat again, harder. "Don't you want to fuck me?"

"Oh, I very much want to fuck you, Bonnie." The simple sincerity in his voice makes me hot all over, but especially between the thighs. His eyes hold onto mine for a long moment before they flash back to the road. "But I've got to say, you aren't what I expected."

Almost unconsciously, I touch a hand to my hair. "What do you mean?" Am I unattractive compared to my pictures? But, no, I dolled myself up today. What the heck?

"You make such a big deal about never having had sex before," he replies, and I relax slightly. But only slightly. So he still finds me hot, but suspicious. Great. "You talk about being a virgin, and yet, you seem so eager for me to fuck you right here and now. Almost desperate."

Those eyes are so damn mesmerizing. I can't look away, even though I feel my body tensing with nerves. Thankfully, he has to look at the road again soon, and I take a moment to catch my breath. "I . . ." I shake my head, force myself out of the trance. "I just want to get this over with. It's business, right? You pay me, I give you what you want. End of story."

"What if I don't want this to be over yet?" he counters, and I blink in surprise. "I told you, Bonnie. I want to savor this meal." He reaches across the gear shift and runs his palm along my thigh. Every muscle in my body tenses, every nerve ending starts to fire on high. "I want you to enjoy this as much as I do," he says, his voice a low, throaty growl, and I can scarcely think straight for the ache in my groin.

I want him. Bad. But fuck if I'm going to let on. He's about a million miles too cocky as it is. "We had an agreement," I say, my voice forced, businesslike. "You pay me, you fuck me, and we part ways. That's what we agreed."

Shit. What if he's been playing me all along? What if he doesn't intend to pay me at all, or what if he wants to drag this out for ages, make me beg for it, make me suck him and fuck him over and over without giving me a cent? My palms tingle with sweat and I clench them to try and distract myself.

I need that money. It's the whole reason I got into this mess in the first place. He might think I'm some naive idiot because I'm virginal, but hell if I'm going to let him get away with using me for free. Especially after that blowjob.

Fucking hell, Bonnie, I scold myself. I gave him that for free. No wonder he wants to walk away now. He thinks I'll let him do the same with everything. Give him an inch and he wants to take a mile.

Granted, I enjoyed the fuck out of it, but that's not the point.

I cross my arms over my chest, protective. "How do I know you're even sincere about this? You could be anyone. That waiter could've been a friend in on this gig."

I jolt against the seat belt as the car suddenly veers off the main drag. He pulls us onto the nearest side-street and whips into a parallel parking spot so fast I barely have time to catch my breath.

Shit. I've done it now. Pissed off this crazy guy I don't even know, all while I'm trapped in his car. I dig my hands into the seat belt, ready to throw it off and make a break for it if I need to.

He turns to face me, and his eyes blaze with heat, though the rest of his expression remains calm. Is he angry, or just annoyed that a business deal is going sour? I can't read him yet.

"When did I ever give you reason to doubt me, Bonnie?" he asks, his voice calm and even. "Our agreement never stipulated a timeline."

Even though there aren't any cars passing by, and the streetlights on this side-street are dimmer than usual, there's enough light from the illuminated sign above a closed corner store for me to make out his flashing eyes. It lights the side of his face, highlighting the sharp curve of his cheekbone as he faces me.

I remind myself that I have just as much of a right to be worried as he does. "No, we didn't," I agree, "But our agreement never stipulated that I'd give you a free blowjob in public, either." My face flames as I say that out loud, but to judge by the faint curve of his mouth, he enjoys hearing me say it.

"You seemed to be enjoying yourself." He leans in closer.

"I hated to put a damper on the mood just to bring up contractual obligations."

I set my jaw firmly. "Well, I should've . . . I mean . . . How *do* I know you're for real about this? That you aren't just . . ."

"Taking what I want for free?" he asks, and his breath ghosts across my lips. He's closed the gap between us. Or maybe I did. I think I'm leaning toward him. I tighten my muscles, force myself to grip the seat belt, the edges digging into my palms to keep me thinking straight.

"Exactly. It's nothing personal, Pierce. It's business."

"Oh, I agree." His fingertips skim my cheek, and the feeling of his rough skin against mine makes me jolt in surprise. I hadn't seen him reach for me until I felt his hot skin against my cheek. He traces the edge of my jawline, and every fiber in my body urges me to lean closer to him, to fall into those soft, sharply curved lips. His smile looks deadly, but I want him to devour me anyway. "But that's something you should learn about me, Bonnie."

His eyes drift over my body, and I find mine doing the same, studying the outline of his muscular chest through his dress shirt, and the thick bulge in his pants. I can still remember the way he tastes, salt and heat, and the way he felt in my mouth, solid muscle but velvety smooth all at once, thrusting into my throat as he claimed my mouth for his own. My heart speeds up.

"In business," he adds, "I always get what I want."

His hand drips down my neck, his fingers curving around the back of my neck to pull me closer to him, and there's no use fighting this. I am putty in his hands, his to control. His mouth pauses an inch from mine and I'm nearly panting with effort at holding myself back. I want nothing more than to close the breath of a gap between us and crush my mouth to his, kiss him, let him taste me, claim me.

But to judge by the soft hiss of breath that he intakes, and the way his eyes flash when I look back up, he's affected too. He wants me. Bad.

"I respect your forthrightness, though, Bonnie. You know what you want too." He's only smirking a little bit as he says that, but I narrow my eyes anyway. Damn him. He knows just how hot he makes me, and he's enjoying it. "So, fine. If this is what you want, we can do this, right here." His hand leaves my neck, slides down my body to grasp my tits through my shirt. His thumb finds my nipple and massages it in slow circles, until it starts to harden beneath his touch. "Beg me to do it, and I'll fuck you until you're screaming."

My eyes dart past him, to the car windows and the relatively deserted street beyond. But there are still lights, still the occasional taxi rolling past, light on, searching for fares. So exposed . . .

More exposed than I was on a rooftop crouching under his dining table? I remind myself.

"I'll send you the money right now, and you can give up your virginity to me right here on this side street. Is that what you want?"

I grimace, debating. I do want the money. But this is starting to feel too familiar. Too much like the bleachers at prom, on a hard floor in a dingy dress, no preparation, no planning ahead . . .

Then again, Pierce isn't anything like my meek prom date. He'll make it last no matter where we are, of that much I'm sure.

Like he's reading my mind, he drops his hands to my waist, then over my hips, one grasping my ass, hard enough that it hurts. I gasp faintly. "I would have thought you'd want it to be special. You waited this long, after all. And I'm paying you quite a sum." The hand gripping my ass drops to the hem of my dress, then slips beneath it. His rough hands glide up my bare skin, and I can hardly think from the red hot flames that his touch sends throughout my body. "But maybe you're sick of waiting," he breathes against my mouth, his lips so fucking close to mine. "Maybe you just want to get this over with. You want my cock inside you, don't you, Bonnie? You want me to claim you, right now. Maybe I'll give you what you want, then."

His other hand tangles in my hair, and suddenly he's pulling me across the center console, onto his lap. He grips my ass again, hard, and I can feel that throb of desire straight down into my clit. He tilts my head to one side, and trails his tongue along the edge of my ear. When he speaks again, his whisper is right beside my ear. "Or maybe I'll just have you suck my cock again. You liked that, didn't you, you dirty girl." He slaps my ass now, lightly, but hard enough to make me jump in his lap. I feel his cock press against my thigh, and I curl my hips under me to grind against him.

"You are a naughty thing, aren't you." His eyes meet mine, and without thinking, without planning to, I close the distance between us and kiss him, hard.

For a second, we both freeze. I'm as surprised as he is, I think. But he doesn't lose his stride for long. He tightens his grip on my hair, pulls my body against his as he deepens the kiss. His tongue parts my lips and slides into my mouth, tasting me, controlling me. I surrender to him with a shiver of delight.

I haven't had enough of his mouth, not nearly, but he's already pulling away, kissing along my neck, down to my collarbone. My head falls back on my shoulders and I groan softly through my teeth.

"You like it when I take control, Bonnie."

"Yes," I murmur, before I lean in to kiss the side of his

jaw. His stubble scratches my cheek, my lips, as I kiss my way along his neck, but I love the roughness.

His hand comes down in a sharper slap, right across my ass, and I inhale sharply. "Yes what?" he says, his voice dark with warning. I can feel myself grow wet in anticipation.

"Yes, sir," I reply, my voice barely audible.

He smiles. "Good girl." Then he tilts my head back so my neck is exposed, and pushes my dress down far enough to expose every inch of my cleavage. An inch to either side and he'd have my breasts on full display to the whole street around us, but I'm too lost in the sensations to care. "Or should I say, bad girl." He raises an eyebrow at me. "Has anyone ever called you a slut, Bonnie?"

I almost laugh at the idea. Then I catch his eye, and realize he's serious. "No, sir," I respond.

"Do you like the sound of it?" His hand leaves my ass to slip under my dress and explore my breast, my bare skin against his palm this time. "When I call you my little slut, does that get you wet?"

I swallow hard. "Y-yes, sir," I stammer. Because holy hell, does it ever.

He grins. "Good. Because I really think you ought to know, Bonnie . . ." He pinches my nipple suddenly, roughly enough that it stings and aches with pleasure at the same time. He pulls it gently, and the pain arcs up my spine. "You are the sexiest little cum slut I have ever had the pleasure of corrupting."

"Thank you, sir." I reach between us, empowered by the heat in his voice, and trace the outline of his cock. I want him, dammit. Fuck our deal, fuck what he owes me; I'm too lost in this moment to care. His lips find mine again, and I sink into that kiss, surrendering. Fuck, does it feel good to let go.

I'm so distracted by the feeling of his soft lips against mine, contrasted by the rough brush of his stubble on my cheek, that I don't even notice his hands close around my wrists. Not until he pulls my arms behind me, anyway, and folds both of my narrow wrists into one of his strong hands. My eyes go wide, but he just grins at me as he leans in to kiss my chest again, his tongue inching toward my nipple.

"God you are fucking exquisite," he breathes against my skin. My head falls back as his tongue laps roughly across my already-hard nipple, then circles the areola, before his teeth graze the very tip of my breast, making me gasp.

"You're mine, Bonnie," he growls. He licks hard at my breast. I moan something between pleasure and agreement. "Say it."

My head swims with pleasure, but I manage to find my tongue. "I'm yours, sir."

His free hand, the one not restraining my wrists, slides between us to cup my crotch. His eyes meet mine, serious and dark in the dim light of the car. "Whose pussy is this?"

"Yours," I manage to reply, lost in the sensation of his fingers cupping my lips.

Without warning, he slaps my mound, hard enough that I flinch.

"Sir," I gasp, realizing my mistake.

In response, he shoves my panties aside roughly, and spreads my pussy with two fingers. Another finger toys at my entrance, sliding up and down my wet slit, circling my lips. But he doesn't enter me. Not yet.

"Say it again," he orders.

I meet his eyes and feel my heartbeat triple, pounding against my ribcage. "It's your pussy, sir."

He smiles. His finger presses harder against me, slick and wet. He's right at my entrance, and my hips buck in desperation. I want his finger inside me, I want him to take me. But he holds back, for some reason.

I groan in desperation.

"What do you say, my little slut?" he commands.

"Please, sir."

"That's it." His smile widens. "Beg for me, Bonnie. Tell me what you want."

"I want . . . you," I pant.

But he shakes his head. "In detail, my lovely little slut. Tell me you want me to finger-fuck you. Tell me how badly you want to come on my hand."

"Please, sir. Let me come for you."

His finger slides inside me, and every nerve ending on my body fires. I try to thrust against him, push his finger deeper, but he holds me back, his hips preventing mine from moving, his other hand still tight around my wrists, restraining me. I'm helpless in his grasp, half naked with my dress pulled down and hiked up, spread on his lap in a parked car in the middle of the street like . . . well, like a slut. And I fucking love it.

"Oh fuck. Faster," I gasp.

"Only if you promise to come for me, my gorgeous little tease." He kisses my neck, the sensitive spot just beneath my ear, as his finger finally pushes all the way inside me. I buck against him.

"I want to come for you, sir. Please, make me come. Fuck me . . ." I barely even hear myself talking now, I'm so lost in sensation. His finger glides out of me, thrusts back in, finding a rhythm, and I sway against him.

He adds a second finger, and I moan in response, my pussy tightening around his thick, strong fingers. He fucks me faster, and his thumb brushes across my clit, sending waves of pleasure rocking through my entire body. I moan again, unable to form words as he pulls me against his strong, solid body.

He releases my wrists, and I grab onto his shoulders for support as he wraps his other hand in my hair, forces me to look him in the eyes. I can hardly keep mine open, as he thrusts his fingers into me faster, harder, his thumb now grazing my clit with every thrust. I feel full to bursting, ready to lose my mind, and he catches my eye, seeming to stare right through me, into my very core. He knows me better than I know myself, I think for a confused, blazing instant.

Then he says, "Come for me, Bonnie," and I don't see or hear anything else.

I cry out as the pleasure peaks inside. My whole body shakes against his, but he's holding me tight, keeping me upright, and all the while, he doesn't stop thrusting into me, circling my clit, making my head swim and my pussy clench hard with every spasm of ecstasy. I feel that orgasm all the way down to the tips of my fingers and toes, as if my whole body just lit up with electricity.

When I finally stop coming, I'm panting for breath, trembling. But he's not finished yet. He keeps stroking me, slower now, his touch ever so light against my sensitive clit. Before long I feel myself clenching again, my body shaking as another orgasm hits me. I shout his name, and he grabs my hair with his other hand, pulls my mouth to his and crushes his lips to mine in a rough kiss.

Our tongues are intertwined, and I've lost all track of time and place. He let go of my wrists, so I wrap my arms around his neck and pull him closer. My hands tangle in his hair. He breaks away from the kiss, and I gasp in protest. But he's only gone a second, leaning over to tap the glove compartment. Then he's back, and his finger is toying with my clit again.

That's when I feel cool metal slide between us. I glance down, my eyes widening.

"Did you think I was finished with you already?" Pierce smirks as he presses the egg-shaped metal orb against my mound. He circles it slowly, and the cold of the metal makes me shiver. "I've only just gotten started, Bonnie."

I swallow hard. "Is that . . . ?"

In response, he parts my pussy lips again and slides the egg closer to my opening. "A remote-controlled vibrator, yes."

I swallow again. Though I can't disguise my quick breath or the way my pussy clenches in anticipation. I'm still so fucking thirsty, dammit. And he knows it.

Pierce smirks as he presses the vibrator against my entrance. It's thick—not as thick as his cock, but close to it. My lips part in a groan as he forces it inside me. My pussy is tight from all the orgasms, but he's patient. And persistent.

As he slowly presses the toy inside me, he goes back to licking and sucking at my breasts, his teeth grazing my sensitive nipples every so often, making me jump and tense.

Finally, he slides the egg all the way into my pussy. I feel tighter and fuller than ever. This is thicker than any vibrator I've ever used on my own. I expect him to turn it on, but instead, he slides me off his lap and back into my seat beside him.

He's breathing fast, too, and the bulge in his pants is huge, straining. He locks eyes with me, smiling knowingly, as he lifts his hand to his lips and slowly licks my juices from his fingers.

I swallow hard, still trying to orient myself. Fucking hell. I didn't know it could feel like that. I've masturbated, of course, but never that roughly, or for that long . . . And I still feel full, stuffed with the vibe he put in me.

He's still watching me, hungry, excited, and I can't help myself. I reach across the console and grab his cock again, my hand curling around his thick, excited length.

But he pushes my hand away and starts the car.

I lean back in my seat, confused, and a little stung. "So you can get me off, but I can't return the favor?" I ask.

In response, he switches on the vibrator.

I cry out as it starts. He positioned it right against my G-spot, damn him. It's all I can do to sit up straight now, as it feels like my pussy is on fire with pleasure.

"I told you, Bonnie. You're my little cum-slut. Which means tonight, it's your job to come for me, and nothing more. Now." He turns the key in the ignition, as I pant for breath. "Which way am I going?" He smiles at me, enjoying my torment.

I grit my teeth and manage to answer with a direction. Then I lose my voice again, gasping in pleasure.

The whole ride is like that. I lose track of how often I come. Eventually I'm leaning against the door, unable to sit up straight, this feels so intense. Every now and then, usually when he asks me for further directions and I actually manage to respond, he taps the remote he keeps clutched in his hand, and the vibrator amps up again.

By the time we pull up outside my place, I've soaked through my panties, this dress, probably the seat beneath me too. I can't even tell. I'm shaky and still yelling in another long, drawn-out orgasm, the pleasure so intense it borders on pain now, as the car pulls to a stop.

"This is you, Bonnie," he says, and I stare at him, wide-eyed. Surely he can't expect me to get out of the car right now. Like this.

But he just smiles. "I'll see you soon."

I reach between my legs to pull the vibrator out, but he catches my wrist, and locks eyes with me.

"Leave it in until you get inside," he orders.

I swallow hard. Stare him down. Is he serious?

He looks it.

So I climb out of the car on shaking legs. I don't know how I manage to stay upright, especially when I'm halfway to the door and he starts making it pulse—on off on off, over and over with every step I take. I fumble my keys a few times, glare at him over my shoulder, but eventually I manage to get inside. Once I'm there, I must be out of range, because the vibrations stop all at once.

I lean against my closed door, listening to his car drive away, waiting for my heart to stop racing and my pussy to stop pulsing and for sensation to return to my extremities.

Only once my blood returns to my head do I realize that I didn't even ask him about paying me again. I couldn't think about business, not with all those mind-blowing orgasms taking control.

This is business, yes. And he's still winning.

Fuck. I am in so over my head.

6

____

"Right, Miss Slutty McSlut-Slut, out with it."

I squint through a mess of curly bedhead hair at Erin. She's bouncing around the tiny kitchen, boiling water for coffee and burning some scrambled eggs at the same time. "Huh?"

She rolls her eyes. "Yeah, right. Don't play the innocent act with me; I've tried it way too many times myself for that to work. Sit," she adds, sternly, and I take a seat at the two-person countertop we use for a mail holder and occasional breakfast stand. She plops a plate of congealing eggs in front of me, along with two slices of toast, one overburnt and the other barely cooked. Yeah, okay, we could use a new toaster. And maybe a better frying pan while we're at it.

But I'm too exhausted to even contemplate making food for myself right now, so I dig in with a nod of thanks. "Not sure what you mean," I try through a mouthful of toast, even though I know by now it's a futile effort.

Erin rolls her eyes exaggeratedly, a gesture she has perfected over the years. "You came home at like, one in the morning last night. After getting all dolled up around noon, no less, for your secret internet date. Come on, do you think I'm dumb? When was the last time you were out that late without me?"

"Uh, every night that I work?" I point out, taking a swallow of the coffee she drops in front of me next.

"Okay, fine, when was the last time you were out that late without me *on your night off*?" she clarifies.

I shrug one shoulder and dig into the eggs. "I went out to eat." I can't do this with her. She'll ask a million and one questions, won't let up until I give her details, and the minute she asks me where we met, what am I supposed to say? *Oh hey, I took your advice and signed up for that sketchy site you mentioned where people auction off their virginity. He bought mine. Oh, right, because also, I lied about prom, I'm still a virgin. And, he still hasn't even paid me and I already did way more with him than I planned to . . .*

"Out to eat. Alone?" She raises her eyebrow.

Okay, so most of my reasons for not talking is because I'm afraid where all this will lead. But part of me might enjoy torturing her too. Just a little bit. "No," I say, trying to hide my smirk. If she won't let up, I can at least throw her off the scent.

"Ugh, you're the worst!" She throws up her hands. "What is he, some kind of spy? Is he part of a secret government organization here to investigate me, is that why you can't tell me anything?"

"He's not spying on you, don't worry." I grin.

"So he's spying on someone." She makes a fake pondering face, scratching her chin in exaggeration. "Oh, is it Mrs. Bishop on second? She's always seemed sketchy to me. Like, she has a Greek accent but she speaks Croatian? What's the deal there?"

"I'm pretty sure she *is* Croatian," I point out.

Erin waves me off. "Where even is Croatia anyway? Is that a real place? Did she invent it as a cover story while she's here to spy on local university students?"

"Yes, because The Fashion Institute of Design is just a hotbed of spy-worthy political conspiracy theorists."

"Girl, you have no idea," she deadpans, and we both laugh. Then she plops down in the seat beside me with a sigh. "Come on, though, seriously. Why don't you want to share details? I love sharing details, that's the best part of dating! Well, that and the sex. But sometimes even then, talking about it afterward is better." She wrinkles her nose. "Oh, god, was that it? Was he bad? Did you have to sneak out his window at one in the morning?" She pats my hand reassuringly. "Been there, honey, no shame in that game."

I snort. "No, Erin, he wasn't bad."

Her eyes light up. "So you've hooked up already."

"No!" I groan and shake my head. "I mean, kind of. A little. Not really. Just making out." And sucking him off under the table of a fancy restaurant. And him finger-fucking me in the driver's seat of his BMW. And then sticking a vibrator inside me and torturing me the whole ride home.

"Okay, good start. He's good at making out, that's promising." She smirks.

"Good at making out" would be the understatement of the year. I can still feel his hands all over me, his mouth on mine. I can still hear his voice in my head. *You're mine, Bonnie.* And fuck, how I want to be.

When I zone back in, Erin's watching me with a knowing smile. "Very good, apparently," she says, and I laugh, but I don't correct her. "Well, fine, keep your secretive secrets. But this new boy better treat you well, or I swear I will find him and I will end him. That's all I'm saying," she adds as she pushes out of her chair.

The mental image of tiny little Erin going up against rich playboy gazillionaire Pierce does bring a brighter smile to my face. And hell, after the way he dumped me in front of the house last night, with barely a parting word, I can't say I'd hate watching the fight go down.

Though I'd much rather her not need to beat him up. I'd much rather he fuck me the way he started to in that car, drive me wild and fill me to the brink with pleasure, and then . . .

And then pay me and get of out my life, I tell myself firmly. That's the deal here. Nothing more. He's a hookup, end of story.

Maybe it's a good thing he dumped me so summarily last night. It shows he's got his head on straight. It gives me a chance to screw mine on tighter, and stop fantasizing about a one-time thing.

"Oh, by the way." Erin turns back to me and I tense, ready for another round of rapid-fire questioning. How much more of this can I take? But she doesn't lay into me with more questions. She just drops a stack of mail on the counter beside my plate of eggs. "These came for you yesterday."

One glance at the top of the pile sours my mood faster than Pierce's non-goodbye. Because I recognize that return address.

Gram's care facility.

I rip open the topmost envelope, and my stomach sinks through the floor, all the way down into Mrs. Bishop's second floor apartment.

Fuck.

I thought I'd been keeping up relatively well, paying this

off in full when I can and in installments when I'm running late. But the unpaid bill in front of me is three times the rate of last month. I dig through the pile of envelopes, find another letter from them and tear that open.

Shit.

They're raising my premium because I missed too many payments over the summer. I fume, ready to call and argue, but they've included a list of payments below, and when I think back, I realize, shit. They're right. I thought I only missed a month, but now that I think about it, I haven't sent a full payment since last June. The diner slows down over the summer months, without the usual crowd of college kids stumbling in late at night to binge on nacho fries and $5 alcoholic milkshakes.

"Hey, you okay?" Erin touches my shoulder. I realize too late that she's standing behind me, and I quickly shove the letters back into an envelope, shuffling them under the mail stack.

"I'm fine. Just got some notices about Gram's place."

Erin catches my eye, and the sympathy on her face right now is even worse than the interrogation she gave me about Pierce. If there's one thing I hate feeling, it's pitied. "If you need to talk or anything, you know you can tell me, right?" she says, and that just makes me feel even worse.

Because I don't need to talk. I don't need to complain about this situation, or vent my feelings. I need to fix it, once and for all.

I need Pierce's money.

And I'm going to get it. No matter what it takes.

I force a wide smile, and even though it's fake as hell, I can tell Erin won't push me on it. "Everything will work out," I tell her. "I'm a little tight at the moment, but I'm just waiting for back checks from the diner to come in. No biggie."

She opens her mouth, probably to ask what the hell I mean, because the diner has never held my checks for me before. Luckily, a loud buzzer saves me from answering.

"I'll get it," I call, leaping out of my seat toward the intercom. Probably a delivery for Mrs. Bishop again. The delivery guys can never seem to be able to tell 2s from 3s. "Hello?" I ask the intercom.

"Delivery for Bonnie."

Erin and I exchanged raised-eyebrow looks as I hit the buzzer.

"Did you order anything off Amazon?" she asks. I shake my head. I haven't been drunk enough to spontaneously buy anything since the start of the semester, when I accidentally ordered 10 spiral bound notebooks instead of one.

When I open the door to the delivery guy, he hands me an enormous box. I frown at the label, but sign for it anyway, and bring it inside. "No return address," I say, slowly, as a sense of dread begins to fill me.

Shit. Is this . . . But it can't be from Pierce. He doesn't know my address.

He dropped you off out front last night, points out the voice at the back of my head. *How hard would it have been to check the address on the front door? To look at the labels on the buzzer and figure out which apartment B. Taylor belonged in?*

But he wouldn't do that. Would he?

"Open it already!" Erin demands, and I guess there's nothing for it. Incriminating or not, I can't exactly pretend this package didn't just arrive.

I grab scissors from the kitchen and cut into the box carefully. Sure enough, the moment the tissue paper inside parts, I know who to blame for this.

Luckily the box on top is just the dress. Shorter than the last one he sent me, cut above knee-length, a deep V-neck top with a flowing, satiny skirt.

Pure white.

"Wow, did you get mixed up with a bride?" Erin smirks and dives at the box. Before I can stop her, she pulls out the next gift—high heels, at least four inches tall this time, and narrower than the last pair of heels. Also pure white, so blinding it almost hurts my eyes.

He did not.

That fucking bastard.

She keeps digging, unearthing a box set of jewelry next. When she opens that to find a pair of diamond-encrusted wristlets (which are shaped suspiciously like a pair of hand-cuffs, if you look at them for too long) and a narrow choker-style necklace to match, Erin nearly drops the whole box in surprise.

"Dude." She whistles under her breath, eyes still bugging out of her head. Then she spots a little note attached to the bracelet case. "'For my blushing Bonnie.' *Who* did you say this spy of yours was again? And more importantly, does he have any friends he'd like to introduce me to?" She grins.

I snatch the jewelry boxes from her hands, blushing furiously. "He's being ridiculous. I never asked for any of this."

"Is he trying to propose or something? What the hell is with all the white?" She's reaching into the box again, pulling out the last package, which of course is a matching set of barely-there lace panties and a filigree bra.

I grab that from her before she can inspect it too closely. "No, he's just teasing me." Because he is. White for my purity. White for virginal, innocent Bonnie.

If this is his idea of making a big deal of me losing it, I wish I had just fucked him in the car last night and been done with it. Shit.

On the other hand . . . I eyeball the bracelets, which Erin is busy trying on experimentally. I could probably resell those for at least a few hundred apiece. Which will pay back a decent chunk of that bill I just received.

Maybe grabbing the attention of a rich spend-crazy billionaire isn't such a bad thing after all, even if he has an irritating way of pushing my buttons as he tries to spoil me.

At the bottom of the box, thankfully undiscovered by Erin, I find another note.

Pick you up at 7 tonight. He signed it simply—*P.P.*, but even that much of a clue would be a giveaway to my sleuth of a brilliant best friend. How many billionaires could be living in the city with those initials? I haven't googled him yet, mostly because I don't want to know more than he's told me, not until this thing is over and done with. But Erin would not have the same restraint, I know. Especially not if she thought he was mistreating me in any way.

I shove the note into my pocket. "Well. Looks like I need to call out of the diner again," I say, and Erin grins sideways at me.

"That job takes advantage of you anyway. Let me call; I'll tell them you're in the hospital. Dad can forge you a doctor's note if you need it."

Sometimes, for all her nosiness and encouragement of misbehavior, I really do love my best friend.

7

____

At 7PM on the dot, I'm standing out front of my apartment in the ridiculous dress. I feel like a runaway bride on her way to city hall, in the white dress and sparkling diamonds and towering heels. But I also, I have to admit, feel more than a little sexy. The lingerie does something to me, boosts my confidence and makes me stand straighter, curve my hips more sharply as I stand in place.

Just knowing how good I look underneath this dress makes me all the more confident that I look amazing with it on, somehow. And this time, I'm not going to let him get the drop on me. I'm going to keep my eyes on the prize. This is business, even if it is mixed with a huge dose of pleasure. I'm getting that money from him, one way or another.

Preferably in a way that also involves him fucking me senseless with that thick cock of his . . .

Still, for all this confidence, my jaw can't help dropping when the freaking limo turns down my street. I shoot a glance over my shoulder at Erin, who's curled up on our third floor fire escape in PJs, cradling a bowl of popcorn like she's watching the ending to Pretty Woman. I roll my eyes, wondering if she can see it from that high up, but she just waves excitedly at the limo, then shoots me two thumbs up, nearly dropping her popcorn in the process.

The limo pulls to a halt, and a driver in a suit steps around to open the back door for me. I climb into it carefully, and realize as I step in that this is the same limo he sent to pick me up from the waxing salon.

Maybe he does plan to fuck me in here after all.

Pierce is already inside, reclining on the far seat, near the bar. He has a glass of what looks like whiskey or bourbon clutched loosely in one hand, but he doesn't even seem to be aware he's holding it. His eyes lock onto me hungrily the second I climb inside, and I can't help doing the same to him. He looks fucking amazing in his dark gray three-piece suit, the darker gray tie the perfect subtle color accent to the rest of the outfit. His cufflinks, which flash in the limo's lighting as he lifts the glass of whiskey to his mouth, match my bracelets. They flash with diamonds, and as I bend down and move closer to him in the limo, I realize they're tiny diamond keys.

Keys to fit my handcuff bracelets. Cute.

"I'm glad you like them," he says, offering me a wrist so I can inspect it closer. I blush and slide into a seat along the wall next to him, far enough away that we aren't touching, because I don't trust myself this close to him.

"You're observant," I murmur, glancing from the cufflinks to his expression.

He laughs softly. "You say that like it's a bad thing."

"It is a little unnerving how much you notice."

His smile widens. "I think it's a good thing that I pay such close attention. A blessing, really. After all, it's thanks to my keen attention to detail that I found your ad online."

I glance behind him at the driver, but the limo divider is

raised. It's glass, but it looks solid, and it's tinted dark. I don't think he can hear us from up there. I lean closer to Pierce, tilting my head. "Why were you on that site, anyway?" I ask.

"Why were you?" he counters.

But I shake my head. "My situation is different. You're wealthy, smart, successful, hot as hell." I flush a little as his smile widens, realizing what I just admitted. But hell, he already knows that. He must. He owns mirrors, I'm sure.

His amused smile fades, and he rolls his shoulders, almost a shrug. "The girls on that site want money. I have money. It seems like a match to me."

"That's not much of an answer," I counter. "I mean, why go on there, instead of dating people in real life? You could have any woman you wanted. A few, even. Why pay for sex?"

His mouth clamps into a thin line, and his eyes flash. For the first time since I've met him, he looks genuinely irritated. Not just frustrated at something I've done, but annoyed. Almost . . . hurt.

He turns away from me to look out the window, and takes another long sip of his whiskey. "You didn't answer me either," he replies after a moment. "We were both on that site, Bonnie. Our reasons are our own. The here and now is what matters."

"I . . ." I shake my head. I don't want to talk about my grandmother with him, or why I need money so desperately. I guess he has a similar reason, though I can't possibly imagine what it could be, wealthy and drop-dead gorgeous as he is. I sigh. "I'm sorry, Pierce. You're right. And thanks for the dress," I add after a moment's pause, smoothing it with my fingertips. "And the jewelry, even though that seems over-the-top for a second date."

He laughs. "You think that's over the top? Just wait until we get to the actual date."

I lean across the seats to nudge his foot with mine. "No fair. What are you trying to do, make me like you or something?" I groan in fake complaint, but when our eyes catch again, there's a genuine emotion in his that makes my heart seize.

Does he? Does he actually care what I think, and want to impress me?

Or is this all an act? Part of his power-play fantasy, in which I am a paid actor, here in the role of the innocent damsel he's deflowering.

It's the latter, I decide. It has to be.

Otherwise, shit is about to get way too complicated.

"Here we are," he announces, breaking up the moment of solemn eye contact. I glance to the window beside us, and I can't help it. I sit up in my seat and actually squee in delight.

Because there's a helicopter parked right beside us.

"Oh my god are we going on it?" I beam at him.

Pierce laughs, hard. "I thought this would make you more nervous than excited."

"Are you kidding?" I cry. "I *love* flying! My Gram was a pilot, she used to take me up in her chopper every summer over the Rockies—I . . ." Shit. I stop dead, realizing my current situation. I shouldn't reveal so much about myself. And if I don't want him to know why I'm so desperate for cash, then I need to stop talking about Gram, *now*, before I talk myself into an awkward reveal.

"A pilot, huh? That's unusual for a woman in her generation, I'd imagine," Pierce comments as he slides out of the limo and holds the door open for me.

I step out beside him, my hair whipping across my cheeks in the heavy wind from the chopper blades, as someone starts its engine. "I guess so," I shout back over the sound of the chopper blades, flushed. "She's young for being a grandmother, though," I add, to try and cover. She's not. She was one of the first female pilots hired to work a major airline ever, and only because she had experience flying as a vet before that. But again. Identifying information. Don't give too much away.

I run my hand through my flyaway curls and change the subject. "Where are we going?" I shout over the rising sound of the motor.

He rests his hand on the small of my back and guides me toward the chopper. As we reach it, his hand dips lower to squeeze my ass tightly. "That, my dear, is a secret." Then he catches my eye and grins. "Unless, of course, you know how to fly this thing, in which case I'm happy to give our pilot the night off." He lets go of my ass, only to slap it.

My cheeks flush an even brighter red, but I grin back at him. "I'd say yes, but, it's been a few years since I last flew, and if I don't know where we're going, and it's nighttime . . ."

"Good call," he chuckles softly in my ear as we climb aboard. We settle into seats side-by-side, and when he catches my hand and curls his fingers through mine, I shoot him a happy smile, squeezing his palm gently. It feels natural to sit here like this beside him, our helmets on, but neither of us talking through the loudspeaker. We're just enjoying the view, especially once we take off and begin to sail across the familiar landscape of San Francisco, and then eastern California.

As the ride continues, he lets go of my hand and brushes my thigh instead. As his fingers inch higher, I return the favor, trailing my fingertips along his inner thigh. His hand reaches my crotch, and he spreads his palm against my mound, thumb grazing my pussy through the thin fabric of this dress.

I shiver and trace the outline of his cock straining against his pants.

All the while, we chat, mostly about the routes I've flown before. Both of us pretend we aren't groping one another in the process, though every now and then one of us will hit a sensitive spot, making the other one gasp faintly. It's quickly becoming my favorite game; as I relax against him and stroke his cock, his fingers slip beneath my dress to toy with my panties.

He talks about other trips he's taken, and his favorite spots. He insists that the helicopter tour he once took of Iceland's Golden Circle, and the volcanoes that lie to the north of it, was the best circuit he ever flew on. I tell him I'm jealous of his travels, and he grins at me, squeezing my pussy slightly at the same time. "Maybe I'll take you there sometime," he murmurs, and I swear, just the sound of his voice like that, so close in my ear over the speakers in our helmets, could sustain me all night long.

Over and over throughout the flight, he gets me close to orgasm. But every time, the second he feels my body tense, he draws his hand away. Waits for me to calm down before he starts stroking me all over again. I think I might go crazy. To make matters worse, even after I half-unbutton his pants and wrap my fist around him fully, I can't seem to make him get close to finishing. He's way too in control—of everything. It's frustrating as hell.

I'm nearing another orgasm when the chopper shifts beneath us. We're pulling into a landing pattern, I realize.

I disentangle myself from his hand for a second to peer out his side of the chopper, and recognize the skyline immediately, even though I've never been here. It's iconic enough that I think anyone would know it at once.

"Vegas?" I raise an eyebrow at him, smirking. "Did you

bring me here to gamble away all your savings, or just to buy a few more girls to share me with?"

He laughs. I love his real laugh, the one he lets out when he thinks I'm not really paying attention, or when no one is watching. It's hearty, deep, full-body. He shakes his head, still grinning. "Relax, hot stuff. We're here to see a show." He catches my eye, the smirk deepening. "That is, unless you're eager to skip the show and get right to making our own." His hand is back at my center, his fingers wet with my desire. He slides one inside me, so slowly it makes me squirm.

My heart skips, but I tighten my hand around the base of his cock, hard. "You know me. I'm always eager to go. Anytime, anywhere." I stroke him gently to emphasize that point. But his palm has gone still against my mound, his finger unmoving inside me.

We stare at one another for a long moment, as the chopper lands. The engines cut out overhead, plunging us into sudden ear-ringing silence.

"And you know me," he finally replies, so softly I almost don't hear him. "I want to make this last."

Then he's pulling out of me, climbing out of the chopper before I can react. In a second, he's refastened his pants and descended to the landing pad below, offering me his hand. We've landed on a rooftop, I realize as I accept his help and jump down beside him. The cool desert night air whips my curls around my face, and I breathe in deep, savoring how dry and chilly it is. The pad beneath us still sizzles with the leftover heat from the sun, but outside Vegas, in the real desert, night is a cold thing.

We stride away from the helicopter. He reaches for my hand, his fingers still wet from being inside me. But I'm annoyed, so I jerk my hand away. In response, he just shrugs and sticks his finger into his mouth. I roll my eyes and look away, but dammit, he knows that it gets me hot to watch him taste me.

The elevator at the far end of the roof takes us straight down to a floor marked *stage*, where a bellman meets us with flutes of champagne on a tray. He leads us down an empty hallway, and opens a side door, bowing us inside.

We enter a theater like I've never seen before. There are acrobats poised all around the stage—we've arrived partway into the first act, but it's a closed balcony, just two little seats all to ourselves, right out in front, closed off by a red stage curtain from the rest of the world. I go to sit down beside him, but Pierce pulls me onto his lap, and I curl up against his chest, hands wrapped around his broad shoulders. He's still hard. I wriggle a little against him to get revenge, and I'm rewarded with the sensation of his cock twitching against my ass.

In response, he grabs my hips and grinds against me.

We watch the whole show like that, a crazy Cirque du Soleil-esque performance with acrobats sliding and gliding all over the set, moving in impossible ways, their bodies contorting all over. And all the while we're contorting too, teasing each other to the brink and back, over and over. I never knew I could feel this turned on, this desperate to come. I can't catch my breath around him, especially not when he keeps grabbing my ass and squeezing, hard.

Finally, I can't resist anymore. I drop to my knees between his, and spread his thighs. I don't even wait for permission—I'm already undoing his fly.

That's when the lights go up for intermission. He just watches me, smirking, like he knows I won't go through with this. I hover at his crotch, indecisive. I want to taste him again, suck his cock until he comes. But the lights are on now, people could see us...

The door to the booth opens, and I fly to my feet, shocked.

It's the bellman returning with another tray of drinks, this time with a whole selection. Pierce takes a glass of the whiskey, which the man assures him is aged and single malt and a few other adjectives I don't catch, but which make it sound quite expensive. I stick with the champagne, because I've learned from my nights out with Erin that mixing isn't a good idea for me.

"Anything else?" the bellman asks us, once we've made our selections. He hovers at our elbows, like he doesn't have anywhere else to be or anyone else to serve. That, or he saw me kneeling and wants to stick around to embarrass me on purpose. Ugh. I'm bright red, but Pierce just smiles at me innocently.

"What do you think, Bonnie?" he asks.

Damn him. I scowl. "I don't know."

"Perhaps some of the new hors d'oeuvres?" the bellman suggests. "The chef has not released them to the public menu yet."

Pierce keeps watching me. I shake my head.

"Thank you, we're fine," Pierce assures him.

I can tell from a glance across the way that there are other single boxes like ours dotted across the theater. Shouldn't the bellman serve some other customers, check on his other tables so to speak? I know enough about servers to know that he seems uncharacteristically unhurried, totally focused on this one customer.

"I guess I'll try some," I finally say, because it doesn't seem like this guy is going to leave us alone otherwise. He bows and disappears, and Pierce leans in to kiss my neck.

"Don't ruin your appetite," he murmurs against my skin, his breath hot. "I need you hungry later . . ."

I shift on his lap, enjoying the sensation of his cock straining against me as I brush against him with my thigh. "Don't worry, Pierce." I lean in to nibble his ear, and his hands tighten around my hips. "You always make me very hungry," I whisper. "Or should I say thirsty ..."

By the time the bellman returns with the hors d'oeuvres, we're too lost in kissing to even hear him. Pierce's tongue explores my mouth, his lips working against mine, and I rake my nails down his back, shiver when he grabs my hips and tugs me against his hard body.

When the second half begins, the lights finally dimming, I lean around Pierce to discover the plate of puff pastries and some kind of savory meat on skewers. I feed him one half, and devour the other half myself, delighting in every bite. The chef should definitely release these to the public menu ASAP, I think, as we watch the acrobats on stage perform another wild maneuver.

Then I'm distracted once more by the sensation of Pierce's lips on my neck. He kisses his way to my spine, then slowly inches his way down my back. He pushes me off my seat, has me stand before him, and next thing I know, he flips my skirt up to bite my ass through my panties. I swallow a gasp, knowing there's another booth beside ours. But fuck, his hot breath on my ass cheek feels better than I could have imagined. And then his stubble grazes my inner thigh, and I go weak at the knees, leaning against the wall for support.

His tongue laps at the crease where my thighs meet my hips. He traces the outline of me, never quite touching my lips, my pussy, my clit. Then he spreads my ass cheeks and slips his tongue between them, and this time I do gasp, unable to quiet myself.

Fuck. I didn't know this was a thing. I bend double as his

tongue explores my ass, thanking god that he made me wax before all this. He delves his tongue into my ass, and I tense, groaning. Fucking hell. Who knew that could feel so good?

When the show ends, my legs barely function. Pierce stands behind me, and I lean back against him heavily, so he's practically holding me up. He leans in to nibble at my ear.

"You are exquisite, my little slut," he whispers, as a pulse of desire throbs in my pussy.

We're still standing, applauding, and before we even manage to turn around our chairs have been whisked out of the way, along with the tray where we set our drinks and plates. A different member of the waitstaff has appeared this time, holding our door open and announcing that our dinner is ready.

We follow him to a quiet restaurant, with only five or six other tables. It's on a high floor of the hotel, somewhere near the penthouse, I think. The huge windows across one side of it overlook all of Las Vegas, and I spend a few minutes standing in front of them gaping at the skyline, until Pierce rests his hand on the small of my back and murmurs that our food has arrived.

We didn't even need to order or anything. And it's a full three-course meal, each one more deliciously mind-blowing than the last. Though none of them, I notice with amusement, are very heavy or hearty courses. Pierce was right. He wants to keep me hungry for later.

We finish with light, savory ice cream flavors, lemon and thyme and a lavender chocolate blend that makes me question everything I thought I knew about ice cream, that's how damn good it is. We leave without even seeing a check, but I figure Pierce must have some kind of deal with management. They clearly all know him pretty well. Maybe he's a common visitor here—a high roller or something. I hear the hotels in Vegas really pamper all their experienced gamblers, since those are the customers who always keep coming back for more.

Naturally, when we leave the restaurant, he pushes the penthouse floor on the elevator. It makes him swipe a keycard, which he does, even though last time I checked, we hadn't checked into this hotel anywhere. He *really* must be a regular. I start to wonder about the site I found him on.

Was it Vegas-based? Maybe he lives here? Or maybe he's a gambling addict, and the bid he put in for my virginity is just another gamble for him. Spend a ridiculous amount of money to see if you enjoy fucking some girl who has never fucked anyone else before, and has no idea what she's doing. That does sound like a pretty big gamble to me.

I'm still trying to work out what's going on here, why all these people are treating him the way they do—is this how fancy hotels treat all their rich guests? —when the elevator doors open.

We have the entire floor.

I step straight out of the elevator into majesty. Wraparound windows surround the suite, and we're so high up that beyond the buildings I can see the faint curve of the horizon, the desert kissing it, and the full moon rising along the distant horizon. A few stars glitter overhead, though most of them are blocked out by the light pollution of the city at our feet.

The ceiling is glass too, clear as the night sky above.

In one corner of the open-plan suite, I spy a hot tub, deep enough to fit at least a small party of people, with jets along its sides. On the other side is a massive bed, larger than king size, I'd warrant, and spread with sheets and a fuzzy fur comforter so perfectly white that they match my dress tonight. In the center of the room is a brazier, already lit with a warm fire that glows in the hearth. There's a kitchenette too, but it looks empty, unused. Nobody who stays on this floor cooks for themselves, of that much I'm certain.

Pierce takes my hand and leads me into the room.

"This place is *insane*," I say, ready to ask him how the hell he found out about it, how he booked it. I knew Vegas was luxurious, but I had no idea.

When I look at him, however, his expression has gone serious and hungry again. His eyes devour my body, lingering on my curves. "Take off your dress," he says, and I waste no time in grasping the hem and pulling it over my head. I drop it in a puddle on the floor beside me, still feeling sexy as hell in my lingerie and high heels. Not to mention horny as fuck from his ministrations all day long.

"Stand beside the bed."

I make sure to swing my hips with each step as I sashay over to the bedside. I know I look great in this—I can tell from my reflection in all the windows, which at night seem to act like huge mirrors, reflecting us back at ourselves. I watch him in the reflection as he gazes after me, lust written on every inch of his tortured expression.

I love having that effect on him. At least I'm not the only hungry one here.

"Lie down," he commands.

I lay across the edge of the bed and shiver in anticipation. He strides across the room toward me, pulling off his suit as he comes. He leaves the tie on, though loosely, but pulls his shirt out from under it, and drops his pants along the way. I can see the strain of his cock from here, desperate and hungry, and I resist the urge to cry out in victory.

Yes. This is it. He's going to fuck me, finally, and it's going to be every inch as amazing as it felt when he came in my mouth, or when I came on his hand.

Then he drops to his knees beside the bed, grabs my hips, and pulls me to the edge of the bed. His fingers hook under the lingerie and pull it down, expertly, tossing it to the side. My ass hangs over the edge of the bed, my body splayed across it, and I shiver as the cool air of the penthouse reaches the wet spot at my core.

Pierce doesn't leave me cold for long. He leans in and trails his tongue up my thighs, one and then the other, blazing a hot, searing path along my skin. I tremble and I groan his name through gritted teeth, which makes him pause and look up, meeting my eye.

"I've been waiting to taste you since the moment I first saw you, Bonnie," he tells me. Then his tongue delves into my pussy, and I arch my back, crying out. He pulls out again, lapping along the crease where my legs meet my hips, coming back now and again to taunt me, digging his tongue deep into me and then circling my clit, teasing.

My head falls back onto the bed, and my hips rise to meet him. I drop my hands to run my fingers through his hair, and when he doesn't stop me, I clench my fists in his dark, silk-smooth hair and pull him harder against me. He listens, giving me what I want. His tongue dives all along my pussy, licking me slowly from back to front, before he slides his tongue between my lips and wraps his mouth around my clit, sucking hard for a second. I groan, and his tongue circles my clit again, harder, faster.

I lose track of what he's doing as his hands join the mix. One slides under me to squeeze my ass, hard, and the other presses into my pussy again, his finger curling so the pad digs into the front wall of my vagina. He rubs me hard there, like he's beckoning me forward, and my body responds, arcing off the bed, my hips rocking with each thrust. His tongue lashes my clit, relentless, and I can't think straight, it feels too fucking good.

I writhe across the bed, desperate, flying so close to the edge I can taste it. Every time I nearly climax, though, he knows—his hand, splayed across my stomach, feels my muscles tense, and every time, he backs off, his smile widening every time I curse him and wriggle and beg for him to finish me.

Finally, after what feels like forever, he pulls my hips off the bed, hugging me to his face, and licks my clit so hard and so fast, in rapid circles, that I can't help myself. I scream his name as I crash over the edge into orgasm. My pussy clenches around his finger, still buried inside me, and my body shakes with the force of that peak.

But he's not ready to stop there.

His tongue keeps going, if anything harder than before, and it's so much sensation that it almost burns past pleasure into pain. I fist my hands in his hair, torn between pushing him away and wanting more, because I can't handle this, I'll go mad from feeling so much at once, but before I can decide, I crash into my next orgasm, groaning aloud, shaking.

He drops my hips back to the bed, and licks one finger, long and slow, eyes on me. Then, without warning, he presses that finger against the entrance to my ass.

"I'm going to claim your ass tonight, Bonnie," he tells me.

I'm too shaken from the last orgasm to speak yet. All I can do is widen my eyes and gasp, as he gently presses his finger into my ass.

My body is tense, clenched, but he runs his other hand

up my chest to stroke the back of my neck gently. "Relax," he breathes, and I obey, letting go of control.

His finger slides all the way into my ass, starts to glide in and out slowly, and with each stroke, I relax more. This feels good.

Really good, actually. Way better than I expected. Not the way his finger in my pussy felt, all nerves firing and climax impending, but a different kind of sensation, like he's filling me up.

He pulls his finger out of my ass, and I sigh, half in relief and half in frustration that he's done already.

Silly me.

He grabs my hips and flips me over onto my stomach, my ass sticking straight up in the air. He lifts my hips and slides a pillow under me, then I feel a sharp sting as he slaps my ass. I gasp, and try to sit up, to glare over my shoulder at him.

He pushes my shoulders back down to the bed, even as I watch him pull a bottle of lube from a drawer beneath the bed and pour a generous helping across his palm. "If you don't want to do this Bonnie, just tell me and I'll stop," he assures me.

I catch his eye, defiant.

I didn't want to, I remind myself. Before I even met him, this was what I said I wouldn't try. I wouldn't let him claim this.

But I think of his finger inside my ass, and his tongue earlier, feeling so much better than I could have imagined. I think of the way he just made me come, over and over again. How good he makes me feel. How he unlocks sensations in me I didn't even know existed.

He told me he wanted to claim all of my virginities. That's the price he wanted. So if he fucks my ass now, then he'll fuck my pussy next, and we'll be done with this. He'll have gotten what he wanted, and then I'll get what I need.

I arc my hips back toward him. "Do it," I say.

He slaps my ass again, harder. "That's not how a good little slut asks to be taken," he reminds me.

I swallow hard and meet his eye. "Fuck my ass, sir. Please."

He rubs his hand across the spot he just slapped, and the sting fades to a dull throbbing ache. "God, you are so fucking sexy. Do you have any idea what a perfect creature you are?" He trails his other hand down my back, tracing my spine. "You drive me wild, Bonnie. I want to claim every inch of you."

"I'm yours, Pierce," I murmur, and even though I said that last time too, it sounds real now. It *feels* real. I am his, and I want him to take me. Every inch.

He slides a condom over his cock, coating it in the lube at the same time. I turn away and press my face into the pillow, trying to force myself to breathe evenly, to relax. It's hard, when I don't know what's coming. But I remind myself that I trust him.

Weirdly, I trust this random man from the internet. Everything he's done to me so far has felt amazing. Even the things I never thought I would like, like being called his little slut, or having my ass slapped.

His cock pushes at my entrance, and I clench my fists in the bed sheets, bracing myself.

He pushes inside me slowly. I feel him stretch me, slowly, wider and wider, until I'm groaning into the sheets, my voice half muffled. He leans over me, his abs pressing into my ass, my lower back. I feel him climb onto the bed as he thrusts deeper into my ass, penetrating every inch of me.

I cry out again, still muffled, as he finally reaches his hilt. He's fully inside me, claiming me completely.

"Whose ass is this, Bonnie," he growls against my ear, and I pant with effort as he starts to pull out of me. It feels painful and pleasurable all at once, like I'm stuffed so full I could burst, but I fucking love it.

"It's yours, sir," I groan in response, fists tight around the sheets. "It's your ass. Take it. Take me."

"God you're so fucking tight." He thrusts into me again, faster this time. "You love feeling me fuck your ass, don't you Bonnie."

"Yes, yes, yes." I claw at the sheets as he pulls away and thrusts again, my body sliding across the bed with the force of his thrust.

"Tell me you fucking love it," he growls.

"I fucking love you fucking my ass," I cry out.

His hand dips under me, and I jolt as his finger finds my clit. It feels swollen and strained, like a heavy weight between my legs. Just one touch makes me jump against him, as he thrusts into me again, finding a slow, steady rhythm. "You're going to come for me now, Bonnie. Like a good little slut, you're going to come with my dick in your ass."

He fingers me faster, and I buck under him. He keeps fucking me, slowly speeding up, his balls slapping against my pussy with each deep thrust. Before I know it, I'm already on the edge, crying out as I spill over into an orgasm. He doesn't stop, just keeps fingering and thrusting, his cock filling my ass. I bite down hard on the sheets and come again, then again. I lose track of how many orgasms I've had.

Finally, he drops his hand from my clit, grabs my hips with both hands instead and fucks me with abandon. He drills into me until I feel his abs tense against my skin, and hear his breath go hard and wild in my ear.

"Come inside me," I gasp, and arch my hips to thrust back against him. "Come in my ass."

He grits his teeth and groans as he finishes, his body bucking against mine, filling me with his hot cum. When he collapses across me, I reach back to tangle my hands in his hair, and lean over my shoulder to find his mouth with mine. I kiss him, hard, and he kisses me back, his lips parting beneath mine. Our tongues intertwine, and in that moment, I think, I could not have chosen a better man for my first.

He pulls out with a sigh, and I know exactly how he feels. I want to keep feeling that way forever. Utterly and completely connected to him. I am his . . . and he is mine.

I shake myself. No. I can't start to think that way. That's dangerous.

That road leads only to heartbreak.

I slide off the bed and pad across the penthouse to the bathroom. It's every inch as glorious as the rest of the place, and I take my time, finding that it's already been stocked with everything we could need. Brand new toothbrushes still in the cases, five kinds of toothpaste to choose from, dozens of soaps and lotions and even a second toilet with some kind of water spout on top of it that I eventually realize must be a bidet.

When I finish taking a quick shower and washing my face and brushing my teeth, I slip into the nightgown I find waiting on the back of the bathroom door. It's silky and see-through and clings in all the right places, yet somehow feels amazing against my bare skin.

Feeling deliciously sore, yet still aching for more, I pad

back across the penthouse to find him curled on his side, dozing on the edge of the bed.

I curl up on the other side, but only after I pull the comforter over his exposed chest.

Then I lie on my side and stare at the distant window, thinking.

Why did he fuck my ass first? I thought by now, surely after a night like tonight, he would have wanted to fuck my pussy. He said he'd make it special for me, since it was my first time, but I couldn't imagine a more perfect setting for my first. So why delay? Why not take me and be done with this?

My eyes drift shut, unable to remain open after such a long night of sensations. But the question continues to swirl in my mind, restless, even as my body surrenders to sleep.

8

———

I wake up groggy, confused. These sheets feel way too nice, this bed too lump-free beneath me. Where am I?

It all comes back in a rush. The helicopter flight, the show, the hotel, the penthouse . . . The pleasantly sore throb in my ass. I shift a little, and that's when I notice the other pressure—the heavy weight of an arm around my waist.

Slowly, moving carefully so as not to disturb him, I glance over my shoulder.

Pierce has curled up beside me, hugging me tight against his body. His chest presses against my upper back, and his knees are curled behind mine, following the curve of my body exactly. We fit together so perfectly . . . And with his arm draped around my waist, hugging me against him, it almost feels like a natural position to wake up in. I'm just another girl, waking up beside her new boyfriend who can't stop cuddling her in his sleep.

I smile, though part of me feels nervous about what this means, and turn back around to doze off. But the motion must wake him up, because a moment later, his arm slides off my waist, and I hear his breath catch beside me.

I glance over my shoulder again. "Pierce?"

His icy blue eyes find mine in the dim, pre-dawn glow from the windows. Before I can say anything, or ask what he's thinking, he pushes off of the bed, leaping away from me as though he's been scalded.

I listen to him pad across the penthouse. In the distance, the bathroom door opens and closes again. I lay back on my pillow and shut my eyes, but sleep is farther away than ever now.

I listen to the shower run for almost twenty minutes straight. Then the flush of the toilet, and the rush of the sink, and the soft swish of an electric toothbrush, or maybe a razor.

All the while, I stare at the inside of my eyelids, unable to drift back off. Why was he hugging me?

More importantly, why did he run?

I hear the bathroom door open and shut again, and footsteps pad back across the room. I wait for his weight to sink into the bed once more, but it doesn't come. Instead, the footsteps cross to the other side of the room, approach my side of the bed. I feel more than hear him bend over, sensing his eyes on mine. Is he checking to see if I'm awake?

It feels safer to pretend I'm not than to risk starting some kind of serious conversation at this hour of the godforsaken morning. I keep my eyes firmly shut, and eventually his footsteps move away again.

Sometime later, though I can't be sure how much, a phone vibrates. I tense, thinking it's mine, but Pierce answers a moment later, his voice low and hushed. I crack one eyelid to watch his naked body as he stands and crosses to the farthest window. Despite his attempts to keep his voice low, it's nearly dead quiet in the apartment, and his tone carries.

"For how long? And why wasn't anyone keeping an eye on the market prices?"

I watch shamelessly as he stretches his leg out to one side, which puts his bare ass on prime display. Damn, boy is ripped.

"I see. And Kelly can't clean this one up?" He turns to the side, in profile, and the light from a building across the way catches his bare chest and abs, illuminates his cock, large even now while it's limp and presumably a little bit cold from the air in here.

"You're sure." He sighs, running a free hand through his hair. "Yes, of course I can. I don't know, a couple of hours." There's a long pause, and then his fist clenches in his hair, and his face tightens. "Well, it's what you're going to get, so take it where you can." He groans as he disconnects the phone and turns back toward me.

He moves too fast for me to shut my eyes again, not while I was busy drinking in every line of his hard muscles. I catch his eye and blink in surprise, then smile a little, forced. "Something wrong?" I ask, deciding it's best not to pretend I didn't overhear that conversation.

"Get changed," he tells me, his voice deadpan. "You need to go."

It takes a couple of seconds for that statement to sink in. Then it takes me a couple of seconds to reign in my temper. Seriously. After all of this, the hotel, Vegas, last night, he's not only going to not fuck me, *again*, but he's throwing me out on top of it?

"You aren't going to finish this, are you?" I shove back the sheets and sit up in bed.

He must be nervous, because his eyes don't even dart down to check out my body, even though I know full well that he can see my tits through this sheer nightgown.

"Why did you bring me here, Pierce? What is all this *for*?" I spread my arms wide at the penthouse. "You said my first time should be special. Then you go all out on spoiling me—not to mention with the freaking . . ." I wave my bracelets at him, because last night after fucking, I couldn't figure out how to work the clasps, I was so tired, so I just slept in them. "The insane presents, and the helicopter flights, and you'll fuck my *ass* but not me, and why? What's the point? Are you ever planning to pay me at all, or is this all some game to you?"

"I told you, Bonnie, I will pay you when I get what I bought. You have assurances now, surely." He points to the bracelets with a sarcastic expression. "You know I'm not lying about my wealth."

"Oh, so you just brought me here to prove you're rich. Not even because you want to have me here."

"You're being ridiculous!"

"You're throwing me out of your fancy penthouse hotel room at . . ." I flail toward the windows, through which the horizon has only begun to turn a faint pink in the distance, the first indicator of dawn. "Freaking five o'clock in the morning or whatever ungodly time it is, and *I'm* the one being ridiculous?"

"I am not throwing you out, Bonnie. I have work to do. I'll arrange for a car to pick you up out front in an hour."

"Oh sure, that's completely different from throwing me out." I roll my eyes, but only to keep them from stinging. Fuck. Why am I letting him get to me like this?

Because I thought he was starting to care. Because waking up wrapped in his arms last night felt too good to be true. Because all of this does, like a fairy tale that couldn't possibly be real—and now I'm learning that I was right. It is too good to be real.

None of this is real at all. And I'm just another disposable whore he purchased to use however he wanted.

I push myself off the bed and grab the stupid white dress from the floor, along with my lingerie. Fuck him. And fuck these clothes he thinks I like, and fuck this whole stupid joke.

I storm into the bathroom and slam the door shut. But instead of getting dressed, I just grab the bathrobe from the closet and wrap myself in that instead. It's warmer than the stupid dress, and a hell of a lot comfier anyway. I shove on slippers, too, and pad back into the penthouse, leaving the other clothes puddled on the floor in there.

"Bonnie," he says the moment I emerge, but I storm right past him to push the elevator call button.

Damn. It's a lot harder to storm out of a place when you have to wait for an elevator.

"It's business, Bonnie. I need to work."

"Whatever." I toss my head, hard. "I'm tired of you playing with me."

He laughs, too loudly for my taste. I turn around to glare at him, but he just smirks. "Clearly you love me playing with you."

I roll my eyes and jam the elevator button harder. "You're just stalling."

He crosses the room to my side and takes my hand, pulling it away from the button. "Bonnie." He waits until I meet his gaze again, my jaw set in defiance. "I don't have time right now. I told you, I need to work. I'll fuck you when I'm ready, and not a moment before then. That was our deal." His gaze bores into mine, and I hate how much sense he makes when all I want to do right now is fume at him.

"Our deal was that you fuck me, take my virginity, and

pay me. That was the deal, Pierce. None of . . . this." I wave my arm at the room again.

"Our deal is finished when I claim every virginity you have. That's what we agreed." His hand drops between us to cup my pussy, and I tense in response to his touch. That only makes him laugh again, because he can clearly read the desire on my face. Damn him. "You will just have to accept it, Bonnie."

The elevator door dings open behind me, and I pull myself out of his arms and storm into the elevator. "You have no idea how much you're fucking up my life right now," I inform him, just as the doors close again in his face.

It's not really fair to throw that at him, I know. He doesn't know because I won't let him. But he can't just go around assuming he knows what's best for everyone, and what everyone needs. Especially when he has no idea what's going on with me, or why I need this money right now.

I clench my fists at my sides. I don't have time to wait around for him to feel like fucking me. I need cash, now. My grandmother needs cash, now.

I hit the bottom floor, and the doors open to reveal more than a few strangers and hotel guests eyeballing me, standing there in a bathrobe and slippers. Damn. And the car—or whatever my "ride home" means—won't arrive for another hour, Pierce said.

Then I notice the sign by the entrance. *Continental breakfast served daily, 5AM-8AM.*

Perfect. If nothing else, at least I can make Pierce pay for my damn breakfast. It's the least he can do at this point. I storm up the steps to the second floor landing, where there's a buffet laid out with about ten different kinds of hot meals awaiting.

"May I have your room number?" the hostess greets me,

and I turn to smile at her, about to speak, when her gaze lands on my robe. "Oh, please, right this way, miss."

Before I can tell her the number—which I'm not even sure I know, is there more than one penthouse? —she's leading me through the maze of chairs and seating me in a private booth in the corner. She snaps her fingers at a passing waiter, who immediately about-faces and rushes into the kitchen.

I've never seen anyone treat guests like this. Not even in fine dining, and I've covered a few hostess shifts at some really nice places in the city.

The waiter returns in a heartbeat with coffee and tea, both of which he places before me. "Would you like any other beverages?" he simpers. "A mimosa, perhaps, or a bellini, that is a favorite of Mr. Pinewood's, I believe."

Startled at the name, I glance down at my robe. Sure enough, there's a double initial crest embroidered on the pocket. P.P., just like the way Pierce signed that note to me when he sent the dress and jewelry. Pinewood?

But then I think about his screenname. PiercingPine32. Well, that would be even less subtle than I already thought, but hey, it fits him.

The waiter is waiting there, hovering, anxious, clearly wanting to fulfill my every desire. I'm pretty sure if I asked him to go down on me right now, he would. I almost laugh out loud, to think it. Pierce is turning me into a dirty girl after all. But there is one thing this waiter can tell me that I want to know.

I lean forward against the table and wrap my hands around the warm coffee mug he brought me. "Why are you being so helpful?" I ask. "I mean, do you do this for all of your customers, or . . ."

His face flushes, but he bobs his head again, clearly torn

between embarrassment and wanting to give me the right answer, whatever that may be. "We aim to make all of our guests as comfortable as possible here at the Woodland Marquis . . ." he says, shifting on his feet. The hotel chain is fairly well-known, so I figure they must have some kind of rewards club or something for big spenders. Maybe that's why. Then he adds, "But of course, any guest of Mr. Pinewood is a special guest of ours, Miss. After all, we are all here at his behest."

My eyebrows inch higher on my forehead, even though I try to keep my expression as neutral as possible. "And why is that?" I ask, hoping I won't give too much away, or sound like an imposter. After all, Mr. Pinewood's "special guest" should probably know why she's so special already. But hey, if he throws me out now, I'm only out one buffet breakfast.

The waiter does look a little confused, but he answers me nonetheless. "Well, since Mr. Pinewood is responsible for running the Woodland Marquis Company, of course."

My stomach twists into a tight knot. "He's the owner?" I blurt, before I can help it. "Of this hotel."

The waiter's eyebrows rise almost as high as my own. "No, Miss," he says, and I start to relax in my seat again, until . . . "He owns the entire chain."

Holy shit.

I knew he was wealthy, of course. No broke guy would throw around diamonds the way he has, not to mention limos and helicopter rides. But the owner of the Woodland Marquis, one of the largest luxury hotel chains in the whole country? I'm gaping at this poor waiter in shock, and bless the guy for not throwing me out of this restaurant on my ass, or assuming I'm some kind of imposter. "I . . . Sorry, of course. I . . ." I stare around wildly for a distraction, and take a hurried gulp of my coffee. It scalds the roof of my mouth, but I ignore it. "Could I get a refill?" I ask, batting my eyes.

The waiter just looks relieved for an excuse to move away from my table. He bows again and hurries toward the service entrance, leaving me alone to contemplate this new development.

The more I think about it, though, the more it explains. The penthouse suite must be his family's, or maybe just his? I pull my phone out of my tiny clutch purse, too small to hold anything but the phone itself and my house keys. Time to break my google block on this guy.

Pierce Pinewood brings up a stunning number of results. To judge by the image section, they're all definitely him—I waste a little bit of time staring at his chiseled jaw, his perfect body in a couple of candid swimsuit shots by paparazzi, and way too many icy blue stares from the covers of huge magazines—mags even I recognize. Hell, Time listed him as one of their 30 Under 30 to watch a couple of years ago—though judging by his age and the article's date, he's just over 30 now. 32 to be exact.

That screenname just keeps getting more and more obvious, I think with a faint smirk.

But maybe that was the point. Maybe he wanted people on that site to know who he was. Why? I shake my head. The reveal of Pierce's real position in the world certainly explains why he has limos and helicopters and penthouse suites in hotels at his beck and call wherever he goes, but if anything, it confuses me even more as to why he was on the Sugar Babies website to begin with. And especially why he picked me, out of all the thousands upon thousands of girls available there.

I shake my head. Pierce is the kind of guy who would never need to buy a woman in his life. They must throw themselves at him, hoping for a long-term time-share in his luxurious lifestyle, rather than any kind of cold hard cash repayment. I toy with the bracelets on my wrists, then reach up to trace the outline of the diamond choker.

Why spoil me, if he wanted to just buy me? I would have let him fuck me that first night and been done with it, but he preferred to drag it out, turn this business arrangement into something that's starting to feel, to me, like a real romance. Why?

Is this all some twisted game of his? Do rich and powerful men get so bored with being rich and powerful that they get off on buying girls' virginities? Is this just another power play for him?

He's certainly good at those, I learn from the first couple of newspaper articles I browse about him. He's notorious for being a shark in the boardroom. He inherited Woodland Marquis when his father died, and he was only 23 years old —that sends a familiar twinge straight to my heartstrings. But back then Woodland Marquis was a single hotel in Los Angeles, not very well known, and certainly not a name associated with wealth and luxury. In the 9 years since he inherited that hotel, Pierce built an empire.

He poured a ton of money into renovating the place, almost every penny he inherited from his father, except for the money he set aside to run a brilliant new marketing campaign. The hotel took off, and before long, he was rolling in profits. But he wasn't happy stopping there—he bought another hotel in San Francisco, then another one here in Vegas, and soon enough New York, Chicago, Houston. He has hotels dotting almost every major city across the U.S. now, and a spinoff chain in Europe. All because, according to this article, he refused to stop running full-speed.

Most people, the author wrote, *would have stopped at that first hotel. He earned a nice profit margin; they would have been content with that, and settled in to enjoy the proceeds. But not the younger Pinewood. He spent every cent of those proceeds replicating the first hotel. Then he did it again, and again. His business has almost never been fully in the black, because he's always reinvesting, buying up on his earlier successes. It's a risky way to play, in business and in life, but so far for Pierce Pinewood, this style of work has paid off in spades . . .*

I'm still reading when my poor harassed waiter friend returns with a fresh mug of coffee. He drops it off and asks if I would like some food brought to me, but I wave him away. I'm no Pierce. The buffet is fine by me.

I load up a plate with toast and eggs and bacon, then devour that along with more articles about Pierce. The more I read, the more I feel I'm starting to understand him. That drive in his eyes, the way he always gets what he wants. The way he kicked me out of bed at 5 in the damn morning because he had a work call—something that sounded like an emergency, to be fair.

Rich as god or not, this man is a classic workaholic.

Of course, that's probably how he got so rich. But it can't be good for his personal life. I doubt he has time for anything, even friends, with how often he must need to be on-call.

I shake my head and finish up my meal. Right then, the waiter returns to tap my shoulder gently. "They're paging you at the front desk, I think. Bonnie?"

I nod and pocket my phone, wiping my mouth delicately as I stand. "The car is here?"

He nods.

Thank god it's just a car and not another helicopter. Much as I love flying, I'm not up for another adventure at this hour, in this getup. I just want to be back home in my cozy, cramped apartment bed, where I can think about this situation I've gotten myself into.

More than ever, I know I need to finish this "business deal" soon. Because I'm starting to feel something more than I ought to for a customer, so to say. And if I'm catching feelings, I can tell from those news reports that it will only lead to heartbreak.

I stride out of the hotel, still wearing his bathrobe. Hell if I'm going back up there to beg him for my clothes back. I walk straight out of Pierce's world, and back into the car that will return me to mine.

9

____

"What's the matter? That's the third time you've forgotten to move on your turn." Gram's ever-sharp eyes pierce right through my veil of . . . well. My veil of Pierce.

"Nothing!" I exclaim, quickly reaching to advance my knight across the board. Less than a second later, Gram's rook swoops in to take my knight, harmlessly, because I didn't even notice him there. "Crap."

"You're usually not this sloppy a chess player," Gram scolds. "What's on your mind, Bon-Bon?"

I flush at the childhood nickname, though to be honest, it makes me feel warm and fuzzy inside that she still calls me that from time to time. My Gram is a no-nonsense woman—she had to be, in order to fly planes and helicopters back in a day when only men were trusted with jobs like that—but with me, she lets her soft side show. Probably because we only have each other left in the world.

I sigh. The *nothing* defense won't work with her the way it has with Erin for the past two days. Erin has also been on my case, relentlessly, to find out what happened the night I stayed over at "his place." I've only given her the barest of details. No, we didn't fuck (technically). Yes, I had a great time, until he got all workaholic and kicked me out. No, you can't go and beat him up, Erin. Yes, that's him calling me. Yes, I'm ignoring his calls.

It's been three days since I last saw Pierce. Since then, I've fantasized about him more often than I care to count. Let's just say I had to replace the batteries in my vibrator.

But still, even though he's tried to call me three times, every day at 5PM like clockwork, I send the calls to voicemail. I figure it must be when one of his board meetings or something lets out, and he's got me on his mind. Or maybe he's trying to booty-call me at last. But I haven't felt ready to face him again, not yet.

At least, not in person. I've been devouring articles and photos of him online nonstop, like every cliché creepy stalker you've ever heard of. But that only makes my chest ache and my pussy throb even harder. I can't stop thinking about seeing him again. More importantly, I can't stop thinking about the fact that the next time I see him will be the last.

Next time we meet, he'll fuck me. Then he'll pay, and he'll leave, and I'll never see him again. At least for now, if I dodge his calls and avoid him, there's still one last meeting in our future. I can look forward to fucking him one last time. I don't have to deal with our impending goodbye, not yet.

I shake my head at Gram. There's no way to explain this to her without earning myself a beating in the meantime. She cannot ever find out how I met Pierce, or why.

"It's a boy, isn't it," she says. It's not a question. She might be ailing and trapped in this facility for the time being, but judging by the way she's kicking my ass at chess right now, her mind remains as razor-sharp as ever.

"Yeah," I mumble, taking my next move on the chess-board a bit more carefully. "I was seeing a guy. Am seeing, I guess. But I think he's going to break it off next time I see him." That's the closest I can get to the truth.

Gram purses her lips. "Hmm."

I expect the usual advice. *If he doesn't love you for who you are, then he can screw off.* But Gram just moves her chess piece in silence, then leans back in her chair to watch me.

Nervous, I make another stupid move, and she snatches one of my pawns from the board. I groan.

"First lesson of men," she says as she twirls my pawn in her bony fingers. "Never let them distract you from the bigger game."

I laugh, in spite of myself. "What does that even mean, Gram?"

"It means." She sets the pawn down with a click and gestures at me to take my turn. While I'm staring at the board in contemplation, she continues. "There are other things in life besides relationships. Those are important, don't get me wrong. But you need to have a life too. When you have a dream you're chasing, a goal you're aiming for, the right man will come along and help you reach it. Because that's what a truly good relationship is—a partner-ship. Each person helps the other achieve a goal they desire, and together, you make the perfect team."

I move my queen forward to put her king in check. Gram's eyes sparkle with approval as she moves him out of the way. "I do have a goal," I tell her. *Saving you.* And getting my nursing degree. And getting a job where I can help people, where I can take care of other sick patients like my gram, and help save them all. I advance my queen again. "I have a lot of goals."

"That's a good start." She taps her chin for a moment,

studying the board. Then, in one swift motion, she captures my queen with her bishop, and I realize my king is in checkmate.

I groan.

"But having goals isn't enough. You need to work toward them. A relationship is a goal, too, but it can't be the only one, and it can't ruin your attention span for the rest of your life if it's going through a difficult patch."

"We're hardly in a relationship, Gram," I protest. "I barely know him. We only just started going out."

"And yet here you are, despairing that he may be about to break things off." She tilts her head to rest it on her palm, watching me with the same sharp eyes that were just studying the chessboard. "If this boy is the right partner, someone who will help you achieve your goals, then he won't throw that away so easily. I'm sure he has his flaws, just as you have yours—"

"Aren't you supposed to be on my side?" But I laugh as I say it. Because Gram is always honest with me, whatever the price.

"I am on your side, honey, and if the people on your side can't give you a little friendly constructive criticism, then who can?" Her eyes sparkle with laughter, too, though. "I'm just saying, it seems like you're jumping to conclusions. You do have a tendency to do that, Bon-Bon. You don't know he's going to dump you until he does—and if he does, well, then he was never the right partner in the first place, and he's doing you a favor. He's freeing you to find the right person." She reaches across the table to catch my hand, patting it softly. "At the end of the day, that's all any relationship is. A test to see if you match. If you don't, the best thing to do is to move on, until you find the one who does—and trust me, you will."

Her wedding ring glints in the light of the setting sun beyond the facility windows. We're playing chess in the tiny game room, but it feels private, with nobody else from the facility in here at this hour. I glance at her ring, the only reminder of a man I never knew.

"How did you know, with Grandpa?" I ask. She never talks about him. He died decades before I was born, and yet she never remarried, never even took her ring off.

Gram's smile turns a little sad. "When I met your grandfather, we had both just come off tours in Vietnam. He was becoming an auto mechanic in our town, way north of here, tiny little place called Redding. I wanted to keep flying, and I told him as much on our first date. The other men I'd gone out with that summer all laughed at me, or told me it was a waste—that a pretty woman like me was needed at home, making more pretty little ladies and handsome young lads, rather than up in the sky sailing all over the place.

"Some boys were more subtle about it than others. They said being a pilot sounded very fun, like a great hobby. Others told me they'd love to have a pilot for a girlfriend, but eventually they'd need a wife who was, you know, *a wife*. They always said it like that. Like I ought to know implicitly what a wife was. And I knew what they meant, and that was never going to be a life for me."

Her smile deepens, grows happy again, and there's a light in her eyes that I've never seen before. A twinkle, almost. "But your grandfather. On our first date, he swung me across the dance floor at a little club downtown, the only one in town, really, and I told him I wanted to keep flying, and he looked me straight in the eye and said, 'Sue-Ann, that is the sexiest thing a woman has ever said to me.' And he meant it." She laughs softly. "Oh, he loved that I was a career woman. He used to come out to the fields and wave me off every time I had a run. At first it was little cargo runs, local trips, with the only place that would hire me. Then later, a real airline, TransAm, and I was their first female pilot ever. Your grandfather was so proud of me . . . He came to my wings ceremony with your mother in tow, and held her up on his shoulders so she could see me getting them pinned on." She sighs and shakes her head.

The smile fades, and a tear glitters at the corner of her eye. I reach across the table to grab her hand, and squeeze her fingers gently. She clutches mine harder, like she's clinging on, and I hold on too. I'm thinking the same things she is, I'm sure. About my mom, who died far too young, and my father with her. About my grandfather, who I never had the pleasure of meeting, but who sounds absolutely perfect for the wild free spirit that is my grandmother.

"He sounds great." I venture a small smile.

She nods. "He was. He was . . . I could never remarry after that. Rich was my soulmate, my partner in life. He raised your mother, and he held down the homestead and let me fly off into the sunset, and he held his head high when the other men in our town called him a sissy and a queer for taking on women's work, because that was what he wanted to do too, you see? He wanted to stay at home with your mother, to be present for all the little moments. He was a gentle soul, my Rich, and he loved cooking for us all, making huge feasts that would blow your mind to taste. Whereas me, my god, I could barely boil an egg. He used to make fun of me for it." She sighs again, but it's a lighter sigh this time. A happy one. "That's what you need to find, Bon-Bon. A partner who fits you. And maybe you'll want to be the one at home with your kids, or maybe both of you will want jobs out in the world, or maybe you'll both want to raise a whole passel of little ones. You got to blaze your own path. But I'm telling you, no matter how unusual the things you want may be, there's a man out there who wants a woman like you."

I lean across the table to hug her, and she hugs me back so tight I nearly lose my breath. Tears shine at the corners of my eyes. I think about the bills piling up at home, all the petty worries of life. I'll find a way to pay them. I'll find a way to get her the treatment she needs, no matter what it takes. Because I can't lose this woman from my life. She's too amazing.

She's all I have left.

"Now, all this talking has worn me out." Gram tries to keep up a strong front, but she's coughing a little, and her cheeks have gone pale. Shit. I reach over to ring for the nurse, and help her stand and grasp the walker she needs now, just to help her get around.

"Let's go back to your room," I suggest, and then the nurse arrives to help, and Gram is too tired to protest, which I know means she really does need some rest. I'll drop her off and head out while she takes her nap.

But when we reach her room, there's a surprise awaiting us. A burst of sunflowers on the table beside her bed, interspersed with white lilies that fill the room with a beautiful fragrance. Where someone found sunflowers at this time of year, I'll never know. Even more mystifying, is why Gram tears up at the sight.

"Oh . . ." she murmurs.

The nurse pauses beside her, checking her pulse, worried. "You okay, Mrs. Taylor?" she asks.

But Gram just bobs her head, beaming. "Yes, yes, I'm fine. Just . . . Those are my favorite."

"Sunflowers?" I tilt my head.

"They had them at my retirement ceremony." She

hobbles to the bedside, collapses against it a little hard for my liking. But she remains animated, as she reaches out to touch the petals on the sunflower. "They were your grandfather's usual present for me. He grew them alongside our house, and your mother measured herself against them every summer, to see how tall she was getting. Someone at work remembered, and that . . . You remember that party they threw me, no?"

I was only five or six at the time, but I do vaguely remember all the press attention it got. The retirement party of the first female commercial airline pilot. Newspapers all across the country covered it. Now that I think about it, I do vaguely remember the photos of her in her flight uniform, surrounded by huge bouquets of sunflowers, beaming and waving at the crowd.

"Who brought these?" I ask the nurse, but she only shrugs as she helps Gram into the bed.

"Anonymous sender. They arrived at the front desk while you were in the rec room."

I dig through the petals, but I don't see a card. "Maybe it's your secret admirer," I tell Gram with a smirk, and she laughs at that one. But it's a tired laugh. The nurse shoots me a significant glance, and I know by now what that means. Time to go.

"I'll stop by in a couple days, Gram." I reach down to squeeze her fingers gently. "I've got work at the diner, then I'll be by."

"Bring your homework next time," she orders me, in between yawns. "I don't want you slacking on your studies on my account."

I smile down at her. "Never." But she's already drifting off to sleep, her grip going loose in my hand. I gently set her hand down on the bed, and let myself out of the room, leaving the nurse to run a couple vitals behind me.

As I'm closing the door to her room, someone touches my shoulder. I gasp, jumping, and whip around, only to have my heart nearly leap into my throat.

Pierce. Here.

For a moment, all I can do is stare deep into his pale blue eyes, my expression a mask of shock and confusion, I'm sure. Then he smiles, and I shake my head, forcing my brain to function again.

"What are you doing here?" *No, that's not the right question*, my brain chides me. "How did you even find me? Are you stalking me?" I scowl.

He leans against the wall, completely unperturbed by my annoyance. "There were only so many female pilots your grandmother's age, Bonnie. It didn't take long to find the one based in northern California, whose granddaughter still lived in the region. And it took even less time to find out that she was still alive, though ailing and residing in a full-time care facility."

I storm past him up the hallway. "You had no right to barge into my life." A thought occurs to me, and my mouth drops open. "You sent those flowers too, didn't you? You looked up her retirement party articles and saw them."

"You aren't the only one who can use google, you know."

I whip around to glare at him. "What, did you put a tracker on my phone or something too?" My voice is rising, getting the attention of the nurses at the end of the hall, but I don't care.

His smirk deepens. "No, but judging by your reaction, I'm right, and you did google me."

"I didn't follow you anywhere, though. And I certainly didn't barge into your life, Pierce Pinewood," I snap.

"Why are you angry?" He spreads his hands, almost like a gesture of surrender. "I wanted to see you, Bonnie. I haven't heard from you in days. I can't stop thinking about you. I needed to find you."

My heart does that jumping toward my throat thing again, and I realize that it's because I'm glad to see him, too. As mad as I am that he followed me, that he barged into my life and found Gram and probably realizes why I'm so desperate for money now, my body has other thoughts. There's a dizzying, rushing sensation pouring through me right now, a happy flutter in my stomach and a buzz between my eyes. I'm happy he's here.

Damn traitor body.

I shake my head to clear it. "You shouldn't have just shown up here. I was going to call you when I was ready."

He smirks. "You mean when you're ready for me to fuck you? You always seem ready for that."

I cross my arms. "And you never do, so what's the problem? Have you suddenly decided you want to fuck me after all?"

He steps closer to me, and it's suddenly harder to breathe now that we're chest-to-chest, his ice-blue eyes locked on mine. "I always want you, Bonnie." His breath ghosts across my cheeks. "I can't stop thinking about how I'm going to tear up that tight little pussy of yours." His finger trails over my hipbone, and I shiver. Then he steps away from me. "But not until you tell me what's bothering you. Why you dodged my calls."

I groan aloud and stomp up the hallway. "You're impossible." I reach for a doorknob.

He catches my wrist. "Tell me what's wrong, and I'll give you what you want. I'll fuck you right now."

"*Here*?" I roll my eyes.

"They have supply closets," he points out.

"Ugh." I shove open the door into the gardens. There won't be anyone outside at this hour, with the sun setting and the chilly fall evening setting in. Sure enough, it's deserted out here, just me and him and the little gazebo where Gram and I come in the summer and watch the dragonflies hop around the pond beside it. The pond is quiet now, the fountains already shut off for the impending winter.

We walk through them in silence for a long moment. He's clearly waiting for me to answer, to explain. I don't even know how to start.

"Look. It's not that I'm not . . ." I stammer to a halt. Damn him. He's just waiting, watching me with that impenetrable, unreadable poker face of his. "I'm happy to see you," I snarl, and he actually cracks a small smile, probably because I look mad as hell. *I am*, I remind myself. "I just . . . I can't believe you would invade my privacy like this. There's a reason I never told you about my life, and it's because—"

Suddenly, he's right next to me. He lifts a hand to rest his finger on my lips, gently. I'd be even madder, but there's something serious and quiet in his eyes. An understanding. "Is that all?" He looks almost . . . relieved, somehow.

"All?" I fling my arms wide. "Yeah, I should think this is enough, don't you?"

"I understand your situation, Bonnie," he says, and his voice is deep and sincere. "I connected the dots. I know why you went on that website. Why you need the money. Or, well . . ." He shrugs. "Why you needed it, anyway."

I blink in confusion. "I don't understand."

"I spoke to the front desk before I came to meet you," he says. "I paid off your grandmother's balance in full. I also paid upfront for her care for the next twenty years, should she need it for that long. Hopefully, of course, she will recover enough to move home, though. I also added a clause for a home nurse, if that turns out to be the case."

I gape up at him. My ears ring. I know he's speaking English, but the words won't make sense in my brain. "You what?"

"It's done, Bonnie. You have what you need."

I'm still gaping at him when he turns to walk out of the garden. Oh hell no. I chase after him and grab his arm, spinning him around to face me. "Why?" I demand. My eyes sting again, not from nostalgia this time, but from a whole rush of other emotions. Relief that Gram is cared for, confusion about how this happened, anger at him for barging in, but a rush of gratitude that he did, that he forced his way past my stupid walls. "Why did you do this?" I blink hard to stave off the tears. "Why help me, why do all of this for me, give up so much for nothing?"

He pulls his arm from my grasp and grabs my shoulders instead. Before I can breathe, he spins me around, pushes my back against the wall beside the door and kisses me, hard. His hand slides between my legs to cup my pussy through my jeans, his other hand grabbing my ass to lift my hips into his. My eyes still sting, my heart is still racing, but I part my mouth and kiss him back with everything I have. It's hard and soft at once, his soft lips and the hard wall behind us, and we're both hungry, desperate. My hands claw at his back, his shoulders, his hips. He pins me against the wall by my shoulders and claims my mouth mercilessly.

We barely come up for air between kisses, until my head swims with the taste of him, and all I want is more. I lift my leg, and he grabs it roughly, pulls my leg around his waist to press his hips into mine. I feel his hard length against my crotch, and I grind against him, our lips still locked.

He draws back slightly to look down at me, his eyes brighter than ever in the blaze of pink sunset in the sky above. "My lovely little Bonnie," he breathes. Then he smiles, sharply. "What on earth makes you think I'm not still going to take what belongs to me?" His hands wrap around my waist, slide past my hips to grab my ass, hard.

I gasp and arch up against him, groaning with desire. And something else. Relief. He still wants me.

"You're bought and paid for, my gorgeous slut." He leans in to kiss my neck, trailing his tongue up to my ear, then nipping at that soft, sensitive spot just under my ear. My legs stop working, and I sag against him, caught between him and the wall. "Now I get to decide when I stretch out that tight, fresh pussy of yours."

I arch my hips to grind against him, harder, and I feel his thick cock twitch against my clit. It makes us both gasp, and when I open my mouth to respond, he catches me in another deep kiss. Our tongues intertwine, and I wrap my arms around him, one hand dipping down to slide under his shirt. I trace his ab muscles, his pecs, all the way up to his shoulders, and then back down to toy with the faint line of fuzz along his stomach, his happy trail. I follow it down to the hem of his pants, and flatten my palm against his stomach to slide my fingers beneath. He gasps and rocks against my hand, and I grin up at him as my fingers inch closer to that glorious cock of his.

"You are so damn perfect," he murmurs, gazing down at me, our eyes locked.

"Thank you, sir," I whisper, my lips curved in a confident smile. Then I close my fingers around his solid length, and slide them up to finger the tip of his cock. There's a single dewy drop of precum there, and I smile wider at how hard he is for me. "One request, though, sir."

His eyes flash dangerously, but he's grinning. "I may or may not be open to negotiations, Ms. Taylor."

I tighten my grip on his cock, and he twitches again, harder. "Don't worry, Mr. Pinewood. I'll make it worth your while." I tilt my head to the side, and enjoy the way his gaze drops straight to my neck, then trails down to my breasts below, my cleavage only a little on display in the casual shirt I wore today. I love that he doesn't seem to care what I'm wearing, though. I could be dressed in a bag for all he cares—he has eyes only for my body beneath the fabric. "If—no, *when* we fuck," I say, drawing out the word fuck. His eyes flash back to mine, hot as ever. "I want to do it where you live. I want to see your home first."

He pauses. He clearly wasn't expecting that. But I slide my fist along his length, starting to stroke him slowly, and from the tension line that appears between his eyes, creasing his handsome forehead, I can tell he's mine. The same way that I'm his already. "All right," he breathes, and I lean up to kiss him again, softer this time.

Of course he has a penthouse. And of course it's in the Financial District.

As we wait side-by-side in the elevator taking us up to his private floor, all I can think is that I'm going to start getting used to this kind of treatment.

That's a dangerous thought.

The elevator doors open on a tastefully decorated bachelor pad. It's got big windows, similar to the penthouse we stayed in at his hotel, though at least there are gauzy white curtains on these, so we can block out the sunlight if need be. The view overlooks San Francisco Bay on one side and the city on the other, and it's all lights and the chilly fog rolling across the bay. But closer at hand, his place looks way too similar to the hotel. It's gray, rather than white, with stainless steel appliances in his kitchen, matching gray marble countertops, and an open plan loft up above. Down a low set of steps beside the living room, I can just glimpse the bed, which of course, is also upholstered in gray.

It's lovely, don't get me wrong. It just doesn't look like a place that anyone lives, not long-term. It doesn't feel like a *home.*

"You don't spend a lot of time here, do you?" I ask as I step into the apartment. Behind me, he follows me out of the elevator, but remains quiet. I trail my hand along the kitchen counters, and glance across at the living room. There's a fireplace, modern like the rest of the place, but it could be cozy. Add a throw-rug, and some blankets and pillows to that deep leather sofa, and move the way-too-big TV a little farther back from the couch . . . Add some paintings on the bare walls between the windows, maybe some thicker curtains, something patterned and homey, and this place could work nicely to live in.

It could definitely be turned into not-a-hotel-room easily.

I glance over my shoulder. Pierce's eyes never leave mine —he's studying me, waiting for my reaction. I smile at him, but he remains serious, almost . . . Anxious? No way. Not him.

"You seem like a very busy man," I point out, stating the obvious. But even then, he doesn't agree. Just watches me like he's waiting for something. "Don't you ever relax? Take time off to enjoy your home?"

He shrugs. "I enjoy living here."

"Do you? Or do you just enjoy that it's probably close to work?" I glance out the window, and sure enough, there's the now-familiar logo of Woodland Marquis glowing across the street.

"I like the apartment, too," he protests.

I laugh. "For all ten minutes I'll bet you spend in it every day." I step closer to him and prod at his side gently. He catches my hand in his, then twines his fingers through mine. "Do you even take time to enjoy meals? Go on walks, take breaks, maybe . . . date people?" I raise an eyebrow, challenging.

He scowls. "No comment."

I laugh harder. "That's why you were on that Sugar Babies site, isn't it?" I smirk. "You don't even have time to pick up all the hot ladies who would fawn all over you, huh? You had to find them digitally, browsing at lunch in between checking work emails?"

"That's not why." He grabs my waist, pulls me against him. He lifts me up so his feet slide under mine, and next thing I know we're walking backwards, me balanced on tiptoe on top of his feet. I wrap my arms around his neck for balance.

"Bullshit." I lift my eyebrows. "I'll bet you found me in between working on accounts, or in the one half an hour you allowed yourself between day-long meetings."

"Wrong." He pushes me backwards and I gasp in surprise. But I hit the bed a second later—I didn't even notice him carrying me down the stairs. Damn, he's good. He's strong enough to throw me around, position me however he wants. It makes me hot as hell.

I spread my legs in a dare and raise my eyebrows at him. "Right." I lift my chin higher as he crawls on top of me onto the bed. I stare up at him, defiant. "Admit it, I'm at least warm."

His hands trace my sides, slipping under my shirt to reach for my breasts. "I'll say."

I laugh and lean up to kiss him, wrapping one hand around his neck. He kisses me back, slow, deep. Nothing like the frenzied, angry kisses when we first met. This is a real kiss. When we finally break apart, we're both breathing faster, our eyes glazed.

"Fine," he whispers against my lips. "You might be close

to the truth. But only close."

"Oh really?" I nip at his lip gently, then kiss him again. "Only warm?"

"Maybe smoking hot." He pushes me backwards into the comforter. I arch my hips and he takes the signal, undoing my jeans and yanking them off in one swift motion. He leaves my panties on, though, and I wonder if he recognizes them as the first pair he bought for me, at the salon.

"So you are a workaholic." I run my hand over his fresh stubble, and savor the rough sensation across my palm.

"I'm busy, yes." He leans in and kisses my neck, and I fall against the sheets, surrendering. "But have you considered that maybe I bought you just for the glory of fucking a virgin?" His breath is hot against my ear, and his tongue toys with my earrings. "I fantasized about you from the moment I first saw you." He bites down, his teeth digging into my earlobe, and I gasp softly. "I imagined taking you before anyone else could. Tasting every inch of you." He licks his way down my neck, and I run my hands through his hair, desperate to feel his bare skin on mine. But he's clearly going to take his time, and for once, I don't mind. Because I know this is it. He's finally going to give me what I want.

"Have you considered why I didn't get this over with quickly?" His tongue, his fucking tongue, god, he's driving me wild. He pulls my shirt off, tosses it aside, and my bra follows soon after, so that he can envelop my breast in his mouth, kiss and suck at me until it's hard to breathe.

"Why?" I whisper, because I can't control my voice any louder than that.

"At first I wanted to savor you. Corrupt you, slowly." His hand drops to my panties. Slips beneath the hem, and his fingers dance around my clit in slow, teasing circles. "I wanted to make you scream with pleasure, and know I was the first man ever to do it."

I shiver, unable to help myself. "No one has ever touched me like you do, Pierce," I murmur.

"I wanted you to be desperate." His fingers spread my pussy lips, and my head falls against the sheets as I arch my back. "I wanted you to beg for me to fuck you."

"You . . . tease," I manage to gasp, in between jolts of pleasure, as his thumb zeroes in on my sweet spot. I can feel my clit, swollen and heavy with need. He brushes against it, and my whole body jumps, electrified.

"Yes." He grins. "But not nearly as bad a tease as you."

I wrap a hand around his neck, try to pull him down to kiss me, but he holds back. His eyes find mine, serious again, and there's something else. Something more he's not telling me. I think back to what he just said. *At first.* "Then what happened?" I murmur, my body tense, waiting for the blow. What happened? Did something change? He still wants me, of that much I'm sure, but . . .

Oh.

Oh.

My lips part in surprise, as he continues to watch me, his smile twisting into something almost bitter. He moves to slide his hand out of my panties, but I catch his wrist, hold him there.

"You've figured it out," he says, his voice low and constricted. Because that's real emotion in his eyes, in his tone.

I almost missed it, because I was so distracted by fighting my own feelings. But he's feeling the same thing. "You didn't want it to end," I murmur, and I know before I even say it that that's why. Why he kept stalling and delaying, why he wouldn't fuck me that night in the penthouse. Why he threw me out to throw himself into work instead. Why he followed me to my grandmother's, and paid for everything, before we'd finished our deal, before he'd taken what he wanted.

He leans in to kiss me again, roughly this time. Before I can kiss him back, he pulls away again, and this time he withdraws his hand from my pussy, his other hand from my breast, and leans back on the bed. I feel cold in all the spots where he was just touching me. My whole body burns for him.

I sit upright and reach for him, but he cringes away.

"I'm a complete idiot. This was a business deal; I don't get in over my head in business. I stick to what works. I stay logical, focused. But you . . ." He glances over his shoulder at me, desperation written all over his face. "You make me lose focus. Lose my damn mind."

I reach for him, touch his shoulders gently. When he doesn't pull away anymore, I slowly sit up and wrap my body around his. "Pierce . . ."

"I'm falling in love with you, Bonnie. And I know, I know how insane that sounds—we've only known each other for a week, and this was only supposed to be about sex, but I can't stop thinking about you, all the time, even in meetings, and I normally don't . . ." He shakes his head. "But there it is. I've fallen for you so damn hard."

"Pierce." I say his name sternly this time, and he meets my eye. I cup his cheek in one hand and kiss him, slow, soft, deep. I don't break that kiss for a long time, not until I know exactly what to say in return.

The truth. A truth I had barely begun to realize, a truth I didn't want to look at too deeply, because I knew how dangerous it was to admit.

"I'm falling for you, too," I whisper against his lips.

At that, his body relaxes. Mine does, too, all this tension

I never even realized I was carrying falling out of me at once. I think about what Gram said, about the right partner helping you toward your goals. Pierce and I were both feeling out-of-focus, lost. But not because we were a bad fit. We were unfocused because we weren't able to see the obvious truth right in front of us.

We fit together. Crazy well.

He turns in my arms and kisses me again, and this time we both pour everything we're feeling into the kiss. He leans me back slowly, and I pull his shirt off, wrap my arms around him to savor the sensation of his bare chest pressed against mine, finally, finally.

Our hands roam all over one another, exploring every inch of our bodies. I pull his jeans off, and he kicks them aside, his boxers too, while I wrap both hands around his cock and savor the feeling of his hard, strong length. He slips my panties off, spreads my legs, and drops his head between them.

I'm not nervous or scared anymore like I was the first time he went down on me. When his tongue laps across my clit, I tighten my fists in his hair, clench my teeth and groan his name.

"Right there," I gasp as he tongues me, again and again, until the orgasm crashes over me.

He slides up my body to kiss me, and I taste myself on his lips, and already his fingers spread my pussy, play with my clit again, as he smiles down at me. "I could watch you come over and over again forever." He takes one of my hands, wraps it around his cock. "Feel how hard you make me, Bonnie. Feel how fucking much I love making you come," he orders, and I clench my fist hard around him as he rubs my clit, so light and fast that I come again, gasping in his arms.

I have a feeling he's going to tease me forever, but I've had enough. I grasp his wrist before he can start to toy with me again, and pull his hand up to my shoulder. I gaze straight into those pale blue eyes of his. "Fuck me, Pierce Pinewood."

He slides his legs between mine, already rolling a condom over himself, and I feel the hard press of his cock at the entrance of my pussy. Every muscle in my body clenches in anticipation.

"Please," I gasp, and he finally listens to me. He slides his cock into me in one slow motion, until he's buried inside me, every inch of him. I cry out, a mix of pain and pleasure searing through me as he spreads my tight walls. I feel my body stretch to take him in, and it feels so fucking right that it's him taking me, that he'll be my first.

"I fucking love you," I breathe, and he smiles against my lips before he kisses me, hard.

"I fucking love you too, Bonnie Taylor." He rocks out of me, slowly, and my hips rise to meet his as he thrusts into me again, harder. "I fucking love your sexy body, and your tight pussy."

"Fuck, Pierce," I groan, and his smile widens.

"I love the way you gasp my name when you lose control." He tangles his fist in my hair and leans my head back against the sheets, then bites my neck, trailing his teeth over my skin, just hard enough that I can feel a faint sting. "More than anything, I love making you lose control, Bonnie."

I wrap my legs around his hips instinctively, and arch up against him as he starts to thrust harder, faster. Soon we're both too lost in sensations to talk, and I glance down between us to savor the sight of his thick cock plunging inside me. I wrap my hands around his shoulders to brace myself, and gasp as the sensations start to build within me.

"Come for me," he says, his voice sharp with the command.

I moan, long and low, not quite there yet, trying to obey him, trying to get to the peak. He pulls my body lower underneath him, angles his hips so his cock drags against my upper wall as he fucks me faster.

"Come on my cock."

I cry out, feeling my pussy clench hard around him. A few more quick thrusts and I lose myself in pleasure, moaning his name as I come. He fucks harder now, his eyes glazed, hands tight on my hips, probably leaving bruises, and I fucking love that, I love that he leaves his mark on me. He comes hard a moment after me, groaning through tightly gritted teeth, and while he's still thrusting, I lean up to kiss him, hard and rough.

When he's finished, we both collapse back onto the bed, our legs entangled, neither of us anxious to move. He lays on top of me, and I can feel his chest rise and fall, his heart pound against my breast, the faint sheen of sweat on both of our bodies mingling with the scent of sex in the room.

"Holy fuck," I finally manage to gasp, and he laughs, his real, deep laugh, leaning back to watch me as he does.

"How was that for a first time story?" he asks, smirking, and I tighten my legs around his waist, running my palms down his chest with a smile.

"I think..."

He raises an eyebrow, waiting.

My smile deepens. "I think I need a second time, to compare it to."

"Is that so?" He leans down to nip at my neck.

"Mm, I'm afraid so." I tangle my hands in his hair,

running my nails over his scalp, which makes him shiver against me. "And after that, maybe a third and a fourth time too, just to be sure . . . I need a good pool for comparison."

Pierce kisses me, and I feel his smile through our joined lips. "Hmm." He sighs against my mouth, pretending to be put-out. "I suppose I can try to accommodate your demands." He runs his hands up my sides, and I shiver. "Difficult as it will be to obey. I'll just have to grin and bear it, somehow . . ."

I prod his side, fake offended, and he rolls over, pulling me on top of him. It doesn't take long before I feel him start to harden beneath me again, and as we kiss once more, and he lifts me to position his cock beneath me, then guides me down onto his cock, until he fills every inch of me, I realize . . .

This is definitely the kind of treatment I could get used to.

EPILOGUE

"Are you sure you remember it all, Gram?" Bonnie is saying. "It's okay if you don't."

"That's about as irritating as if I asked you whether you remember how to walk," Bonnie's grandmother snaps, though she's smiling as she swats her granddaughter's wrist.

Sitting in the backseat of my chopper, watching the two of them interact, I can definitely see the resemblance. Sue-Ann, as Mrs. Taylor has insisted I call her, might be more than three times Bonnie's age, but she's still a spitfire. Not to mention they share the same emerald green eyes, both of which are sparkling in the early morning sun right now.

Bonnie, for all her fussing, is just as excited about this as her grandmother. And I can see why.

"Go on, get in the back before your man get's lonesome," Sue-Ann orders, and Bonnie leans in to kiss the older woman's cheek before she hops over the seat to join me. I catch her hand as she comes, and pull her straight onto my lap. Yes, I'll let her have her own seat when she needs to, but until then, I call dibs.

I hug Bonnie to my chest, and when her gram turns to

study the controls some more, I sneak a hand beneath her shirt to fondle her breast. Bonnie turns bright red and slaps at my wrist.

"Pierce," she hisses, half scolding and half loving this.

I tweak her nipple, and lean in to bite at her neck, when I catch Sue-Ann eyeballing us in the mirror. I drop my grip on Bonnie, though not before the old woman bursts into laughter.

"Don't bother to play innocent, young man, I've seen it all before," Sue-Ann says, while Bonnie's entire face goes bright red.

She does look awfully adorable when she blushes like that. And it's so easy to make her do it, too. I grin, and she glares at me. Too bad her angry glowering face looks even sexier. It really puts a damper on her attempt to punish me.

"Don't encourage him, Gram," Bonnie says. As she does, the side door opens, and Henry joins us. Henry has been my pilot since I bought this helicopter almost five years ago. I can tell he's a little bit put-out about flying backup co-pilot now, since normally that job falls to me.

"Thanks again for chaperoning, Henry," I tell him over the headset as he revs up the engine.

Sue-Ann swats Henry's hand away from the starter and turns it herself. "Though I don't see why we need *two* pilots. In the war, you know, you were lucky if you had one."

Bonnie rolls her eyes. "Gram, you always had a pilot in the war."

"Not if he got himself shot," she points out, and we all sober up for a second at the thought. "Lucky for my passengers, I'm bullet-proof," she adds, and with that, she grasps the controls and starts to ease us into the air.

Bonnie slides off my lap onto the seat next to me, squeezing my hand tightly before she fastens her belt. I can tell from the little tic in her forehead that she's nervous. I don't blame her. Her grandmother hasn't flown a chopper in years, not since she first started to get sick. But the nursing home released her to a full-time at-home care nurse six months ago, and last month they bumped her down to part-time care only.

"She's a trooper," the doctor told us in the waiting room, after he'd finished her exam. "I've never seen anything like her recovery. Of course, she'll have difficulty going forward, and you'll always need to keep a close eye on her—she won't last forever," he added, probably because Bonnie was looking extremely thrilled by the news.

I could've punched him for saying that, for souring the bright expression on Bonnie's face. But I understand. He's right. We have to cherish the time we have left.

Which is why, against the advice of that same doctor, I spoke to Henry and arranged this flight. It was Sue-Ann's greatest wish—to pilot one last flight before she really and truly gives up the ghost of her old life, and admits she's too old to fly anymore.

Henry made me install all kinds of failsafes in the chopper, controls that allow him to take over at a moment's notice if anything goes wrong in midair, or if Sue-Ann messes anything up. But it was worth the price of renovations to see the look on the old woman's face now, as we lift off the ground of northern California and into the sky.

Sue-Ann whoops at the top of her lungs, beaming, and for a second, I glimpse the way she must have looked decades ago, helming airplanes and helicopters alike, young and beautiful and full of life. No wonder Bonnie's grandfather fell so hard for her. No wonder he loved her passion for flight, and worked alongside her to make her dreams happen.

I wrap my arm around Bonnie and pull her close to me, squeezing her shoulders. Bonnie gets that same light in her eye when she's working at the hospital. She's just starting out volunteering now, bolstering her hours as she continues to finish her classes. I finally convinced her, only a couple of months ago, to quit her terrible diner job and focus on school full-time. She was stubbornly set on supporting herself entirely through school, so it took some convincing on my part to make her see sense. She has a goal in mind: nursing. Any time she spends at the diner or working some crappy part-time job to reach that goal is less time she's spending actually working in what she loves. If she trusts me and lets me help her out, pay for some of her tuition ("it's just a loan," she tells me forcibly every time. "I'm paying you back every cent later"), then she can reach her goal that much faster.

What I don't know how to explain to her, what I always fail to find the words to express, is that she has already paid me back those loans a thousand times over. I don't need money. I have plenty. What I never had before was a home to come back to. A reason to stop making more money, and start spending it. Start enjoying myself.

You can't take it with you, after all. That's what Bonnie and her grandmother are both so fond of reminding me, when they chide me into taking a vacation.

Hell, last month, Bonnie even managed to talk me into a weeklong vacation in the Bahamas. I have never taken a full consecutive week off in my entire life. I probably still wouldn't have, if she hadn't, unbeknownst to me, pulled my computer and cell phone out of my suitcase at the last second and then rushed us to the airport before I noticed.

I grin at the memory, and Bonnie finally notices I'm staring at her. She leans in to nudge her head against mine.

"What?" she asks over the headset.

"Nothing." I lean down to kiss her softly. "Just enjoying the view."

She snorts. "Liar." She prods my chest, but then settles against my side with a happy sigh. I enjoy the angle, not least because of the view it provides me straight down her shirt, to the lacy red bra she's wearing, part of a new set I picked out for her last week. Oh, I'm going to do terrible things to that bra later . . .

But for now, I just hold her tight to my side and watch the late-summer landscape of NoCal drift past beneath us. I never knew I could feel like this. I never knew life could be this easy, or a relationship this simple. Being with Bonnie feels like finally learning how to breathe, after years spent struggling to catch my breath.

It's crazy to think back from where we are now to how this all started. To me and her on that crazy website, just clicking one another's names by happenstance. I saved the photo of her ad on my desktop—I never told her that, but if she ever checks my computer, she's probably seen it floating past on the screensaver at some point. It was a picture of her smiling, those bright green eyes like emeralds, those blonde curls cascading around her face. It was her eyes that pulled me in, made me click. Made me start to fantasize about being her first.

I'd never been one for the corruption fantasy, but something about her innocent smile made me recognize that there was a tiger hiding beneath. I got so crazy turned-on by the idea of buying her virginity, being the first man to take her, make her mine.

I had no idea that in the process, I'd become hers, too. But here we are now, coming up on a whole year later, and already I cannot imagine my world without her. I took her and claimed her, but she claimed me too. I am hers and she is mine, and we make the best damn team in the world.

"What are you thinking?" Bonnie asks quietly. I blink, startled. I hadn't realized she was watching me, but she is, her chin tilted up, resting on my chest as she gazes into my eyes.

"I'm thinking how lucky I am to have met you."

"To have bought me, you mean," she smirks, and her hand slides up my thigh teasingly.

I reach down to take her wrist, then pull her hand onto my cock. I'm getting harder by the second, especially now that her deft, surprisingly strong fingers are tracing the outline through my jeans. "It was a pretty good purchase, I have to say. Best acquisition I've ever made."

"Is that so, Mr. Pinewood?" She leans up to kiss me, tightening her grip, and that's when Sue-Ann clears her throat sharply in our ears.

We glance over our shoulders to find Henry blushing red and staring out his window, and Sue-Ann smirking in the mirror. "You realize your headsets are on general broadcast, right lovebirds?"

"Oh my god," Bonnie groans, as I burst into laughter. "Gram, I can explain—"

Sue-Ann holds up a hand, though the helicopter remains perfectly steady. The woman really is a pro. "I don't want to know what the hell any of that meant." Then her gaze finds mine, and narrows slightly. I feel a nervous sweat break out along my spine, but only for a second. Then she laughs again, louder. "I only have one demand, young man."

"Your demand is my command," I promise.

Sue-Ann grins. "Take good care of her."

I tighten my arm around Bonnie's shoulders. "Oh, trust me, Mrs. Taylor. I will."

Later that night, in the privacy of my penthouse, which Bonnie has already turned into a homier space than I could have imagined, I make good on that promise. Though probably not in a way anyone's family would want to know about.

"Oh fuck," Bonnie groans, arching against my new standing desk, which handily rises and lowers at the touch of a button. Perfect for positioning it at just the right height to bend her over it.

I pause, my hand hovering on the string of anal beads protruding from her ass. She's only one deep, and she's gasping already. "Want me to stop?" I ask, teasing. I already know the answer.

"Fuck no," she almost growls. I love when she gets antsy. She's so easy to tease. I force the beads deeper into her ass, sliding another one, two, three deep, until we're almost at the largest one. She moans and writhes across the desk. Fucking hell, she is so goddamn hot.

"What do you think, my sexy little slut?" I run my hands over her perfect ass cheeks. Slap one lightly, then again as she moans in pleasure. "Do you surrender yet?"

"Never," she pants.

I grin. "That's my girl." I slide the largest bead into her, and she cries out in that throaty, sexy way that gets me hard as hell.

I position myself behind her, spreading her legs and dropping my jeans to run my cock along her slit. She's soaking wet, shivering with anticipation. "Have I told you how fucking hot you make me?" I ask as I tease her, stroking my cock between her pussy lips, up over her clit, then down to her asshole to brush against the anal toy.

She quivers, but glances over her shoulder at me, grinning. "Only about a thousand times."

"Good." I plunge into her without warning, my cock sliding deep into her tight, wet pussy. She moans, and I lean over to kiss her neck. I won't be able to tease her much longer. I'm about to lose control; I want to fuck her more than anything, and I will. But for one more second, I enjoy the view, tracing my hands along her perfect body. "Don't you forget it," I tell her, and she smiles at me, turns her head so I can kiss her sexy, pert little mouth.

"Now will you fuck me?" She bats her eyes.

I grab her hair tightly and slide out of her. I slap her ass hard enough that the beads jiggle inside her. She groans. "Beg," I command.

"Please fuck me, sir. Please, I need your cock inside me. Fuck me hard, sir."

I grin. Well. Who can deny a request like that?

www.ingramcontent.com/pod-product-compliance
Lightning Source LLC
Chambersburg PA
CBHW020959160726
47994CB00006B/2296